Terry Pratchett was born in 1 [barcode obscures text] ork as a journalist one day in 1965 a [obscured] er, work experience *meaning* som [obscured] just about every job it's possible to [obscured] journalism, except of course covering Saturday afte [obscured] football, he joined the Central Electricity Generating Board and became press officer for four nuclear power stations. He'd write a book about his experiences if he thought anyone would believe it.

All this came to an end in 1987 when it became obvious that the Discworld series was much more enjoyable than real work. Since then the books have reached double figures and have a regular place in the bestseller lists. He also writes books for younger readers. Occasionally he gets accused of literature.

Terry Pratchett lives in Wiltshire with his wife Lyn and daughter Rhianna. He says writing is the most fun anyone can have by themselves.

Stephen Briggs was born in Oxford in 1951 and he still lives there, with his wife Ginny and their sons, Philip and Christopher.

In what would generally pass for real life he works for a small government department dealing with the food industry. However, as an escape to a greater reality, he has been involved for many years in the Machiavellian world of amateur dramatics, which is how he came to discover the Discworld.

Stephen is, by nature, a Luddite, but the Discworld has drawn him into the world of PCs, wordprocessing and electronic mail; he has even been known to paddle on the Internet. His other interests include sketching, back-garden ornithology and Christmas. He has never read *Lord of the Rings* all the way through.

Books by Terry Pratchett

THE COLOUR OF MAGIC*
THE LIGHT FANTASTIC*
EQUAL RITES*
MORT*
SOURCERY*
WYRD SISTERS*
PYRAMIDS*
GUARDS! GUARDS!*
ERIC (co-published with Gollancz)
MOVING PICTURES*
REAPER MAN*
WITCHES ABROAD*
SMALL GODS*
LORDS AND LADIES*
MEN AT ARMS*
SOUL MUSIC*
INTERESTING TIMES*
MASKERADE*
FEET OF CLAY

THE COLOUR OF MAGIC – GRAPHIC NOVEL
THE LIGHT FANTASTIC – GRAPHIC NOVEL
THE STREETS OF ANKH-MORPORK
(with Stephen Briggs)
THE DISCWORLD MAPP (with Stephen Briggs)
MORT – THE PLAY (adapted by Stephen Briggs)
WYRD SISTERS – THE PLAY
(adapted by Stephen Briggs)

GUARDS! GUARDS! – THE PLAY
(adapted by Stephen Briggs)

GOOD OMENS (with Neil Gaiman)
STRATA
THE DARK SIDE OF THE SUN

TRUCKERS*
DIGGERS*
WINGS*
THE CARPET PEOPLE
ONLY YOU CAN SAVE MANKIND*
JOHNNY AND THE DEAD*
JOHNNY AND THE BOMB*

* also available in audio

and published by Corgi

HOG FATHER
THE UNADULTERATED CAT
(with Gray Jolliffe)
THE DISCWORLD COMPANION
(with Stephen Briggs)
TERRY PRATCHETT'S DISCWORLD QUIZBOOK
by David Langford

published by Gollancz

TERRY PRATCHETT'S
MEN AT ARMS
the play

adapted for the stage by

STEPHEN BRIGGS

CORGI BOOKS

MEN AT ARMS – THE PLAY
A CORGI BOOK : 0 552 14432 0

First publication in Great Britain

PRINTING HISTORY
Corgi edition published 1997

Men at Arms originally published in Great Britain by
Victor Gollancz Ltd
Copyright © Terry and Lyn Pratchett 1993

Stage adaptation copyright
© by Terry Pratchett and Stephen Briggs 1997

Discworld® is a registered trademark

The right of Terry Pratchett and Stephen Briggs to be identified as the authors of this
work has been asserted in accordance with sections 77 and 78 of the Copyright
Designs and Patents Act 1988.

Set in 12pt Monotype Ehrhardt by
Phoenix Typesetting, Ilkley, West Yorkshire.

Corgi Books are published by Transworld Publishers Ltd,
61–63 Uxbridge Road, London W5 5SA,
in Australia by Transworld Publishers (Australia) Pty Ltd,
15–25 Helles Avenue, Moorebank, NSW 2170
and in New Zealand by Transworld Publishers (NZ) Ltd,
3 William Pickering Drive, Albany, Auckland.

Reproduced, printed and bound in Great Britain by
Cox & Wyman Ltd, Reading, Berks.

INTRODUCTION

Having staged *Guards! Guards!* in 1993, it was of course logical to follow it up with *Guards! Guards!2* (*Men at Arms*) the following year.

We already had, amongst the Studio Theatre Club, some pretty close matches for Captain Vimes, Corporal Nobbs and Sergeant Colon. Also, *Men at Arms* gave the Patrician a much more important rôle (no prizes for guessing who played *that* part!).

Like *Guards! Guards!*, *Men at Arms* does not offer many opportunities for female actors – three, with Angua, Lady Ramkin and our Footnote. Again, there are smaller rôles that may be played by either sex. Apart from the need for a troll and a talking gargoyle, our biggest problem (no joke intended) was the dwarf, Cuddy. In the event, we compromised and had him/her played by a girl (after all, sex is pretty vague when it comes to dwarfs!).

As readers of the earlier play texts will know, these were all premièred in Abingdon's tiny, medieval, Unicorn Theatre. The adaptations were written with the restrictions of the building, and the numbers of players I expected to have at my disposal, in mind. Really complicated scenic effects were virtually impossible. Anyone thinking of staging a Discworld play can be as imaginative as they like – call upon the might of Industrial

Light & Magic, if it's within their budget. But *Men at Arms can* be staged with a very modest outlay on special effects and the notes that accompany the text are intended to be a guide for those, like us, with limited budgets. Bigger groups, with teams of experts on hand, can let their imaginations run wild!

The script as it appears here is now tried and tested, but it isn't the *only* way to adapt the book. Other groups might make different choices. Some might have many more people available than we did, and they might want to add in 'crowd' scenes. What is important, though, is to ensure that a scene left in at one point in the play doesn't rely for part of its humour or logic on a scene you've cut elsewhere – or that a scene you've added as a show-stopper doesn't end up just slowing it down instead!

In short, though, our experience and that of other groups is that it pays to work hard on getting the costumes and lighting right, and to keep the scenery to little more than, perhaps, a few changes of level. There's room for all sorts of ideas here. The Discworld, as it says in the books, is your mollusc.

Characterisation

Within the constraints of what is known and vital about each character, there is still room for flexibility of interpretation. With the main rôles, though, you have to recognise that your audiences will expect them to look as much like the book descriptions as possible. However, most drama clubs don't have a vast range from which to choose and it's the acting that's more important than the look of the player when it comes down to it!

The Footnote

When we staged *Mort*, we'd employed the device of allowing characters to step out of the play to comment on/advance the action and, in some cases, to help to cover for scene changes. By the time I came to adapt *Guards! Guards!* the idea of using Terry's own literary device – the footnote – had been placed in my mind. This allowed us to include some good gags that would have been difficult to work into characters' dialogue and also, on occasion, to introduce a character to the audience.

Our Footnote was female. She wore tights, shoes decorated with spangly asterisks and a long white T-shirt bearing the legend –

*footnote

She carried a long black pole surmounted by a disc with an asterisk painted on it. Attached to the pole was a klaxon. Whenever the Footnote needed to make an announcement, she would sound the klaxon; the action on stage would freeze and she would then walk in, say her piece, re-sound the klaxon to re-start the action and depart. It worked well, and we employed the same device the following year in *Men at Arms*.

Death

On the Discworld he is a seven-foot tall skeleton of polished bone, in whose eye sockets there are tiny points of light (usually blue). He normally wears a robe apparently woven of absolute darkness – and sometimes also a riding cloak fastened with a silver brooch. He smells, not unpleasantly, of the air in old, forgotten rooms.

His scythe looks normal enough, except for the blade: it is so thin you can see through it, a pale blue shimmer that could slice flame and chop sound. The sword has the same ice-blue, shadow-thin blade, of the extreme thinness necessary to separate body from soul.

Having staged *Mort* a couple of years previously, we were fortunate in having 'invested' in a Death costume which was then available to do guest appearances in later shows. We had had Death's head-mask and gloves, robes and weapons made for us to our design by a firm called Creative Madness (now run as Spyder's FX, 2D Veale Close, Hatherlea, Okehampton, Devon). His eyes glowed blue, and the clear perspex blades of his sword and scythe – 'sharp' enough to see through!

Vimes

Captain of the Ankh-Morpork City Watch. Badge No.177. An upright and honest man whose appointment to the Night Watch – regarded by all sensible people as a completely useless appendage to the running of the city – may have been the cause of his drinking problem. But it has also been suggested that he is in fact naturally more sober than other people. A state of acute sobriety is not one in which a man would like to view the society of Ankh-Morpork and he naturally sought to ameliorate this with a drink or five, and got the number wrong.

It is known that he was born in the Shades and would have joined the Watch shortly after leaving school if he had ever gone to school. Vimes never got the hang of ambition and worked his way sideways rather than up, and his promotion to Captain was simply the result of the sheer unthinkability of promoting any other watchman.

By his own account, he is a skinny, unshaven collection of bad habits marinated in alcohol. He is morose, cynical and ridiculously — and to his own embarrassment — soft-hearted in certain circumstances. He is almost certainly one of Nature's policemen; it has been said of him that his soul burns to arrest the Creator of the universe for getting it wrong.

He loathes kings, and hates undead and Assassins. He is also unashamedly speciesist — he deeply dislikes trolls and dwarfs, but in an almost proprietorial way, so that he has risked his life and badge to defend them merely so that he can continue to dislike them. He hates the city in the same way; it's his to hate.

Carrot

(Carrot Ironfoundersson). A dwarf (by adoption). His adoptive dwarf parents found him in the woods as a toddler, wandering near the bodies of his real parents, who had been victims of a bandit attack. Also in the wreckage of the cart was a sword, and a ring that was very similar to one recorded as having once been a part of the royal jewellery of Ankh.

He is six feet six inches tall with a big, honest forehead, mighty neck and impressively pink skin, due to scrubbing. He became known as Carrot not because of his red hair, kept short for reasons of hygiene, but because of his shape — the kind of tapering shape a boy gets through clean living, healthy eating and good mountain air in huge lungfuls. When Carrot flexes his muscles, other muscles have to move out of the way first. He has a punch which even trolls have learned to respect. He walks with a habitual stoop, which comes of being two metres tall but living with dwarfs. Like all dwarfs, when away from home he writes at least once a week.

His adoptive parents, embarrassed at his size and the fact that he had reached puberty at what, in dwarf terms, is about playgroup age, realised that he needed to be among his own kind. They arranged for him to join the Night Watch in Ankh-Morpork because, they had been told, it would make a man of him.

Being very literal-minded is a dwarfish trait. It is one which Carrot shares. In the whole of his life (prior to his arrival in Ankh-Morpork) no-one ever really lied to him or gave him an instruction that he wasn't meant to take literally. He is direct, honest, good-natured and honourable in all his dealings. Despite a full year in the Watch he still thinks everyone is decent underneath and would get along just fine if only they made the effort. He is genuinely, almost supernaturally likeable. And he is astonishingly simple – which is not at all the same as 'stupid'. It is just that he sees the world shorn of all the little lies and prevarications that other people erect in order to sleep at night.

After a few initial setbacks, Carrot has had an exemplary career as a policeman, often helped by the fact that people confuse his simplicity with idiocy.

He has a crown-shaped birthmark at the top of his left arm. Coupled with his sword, his charisma, his natural leadership, and his deep and almost embarrassing love of Ankh-Morpork, this rather suggests that he is the long-lost rightful heir to the throne of the city.

He seriously believes that to be a policeman is to be the guardian of civilisation. He is, in fact, very happy in his job.

Colon

Sergeant in the Ankh-Morpork City Watch. Age believed to be about sixty. A fat man with a huge, red face like a harvest moon. He is married with three grown-up children, and some grand-children. He likes the peace and quiet of the night; he owes thirty years of happy marriage to the fact that Mrs Colon works all day gutting fish and he works all night.

Fred Colon used to be in an army (city unknown) but has been in the City Watch for thirty years, and he has known Captain Vimes for over twenty years. He smokes a pipe, and wears sandals with his Watch uniform, along with a breastplate with impressive pectoral muscles embossed on it, which his chest and stomach fit into in the same way that jelly fits into a mould.

He is the sort of man who, in a military career, will automatically gravitate to the post of sergeant. As a civilian, his natural rôle would be something like a sausage butcher – some job where a big, red face and tendency to sweat even in frosty weather are practically part of the specification.

Nobby

Corporal C.W.St J. (Cecil Wormsborough St John). A corporal in the Ankh-Morpork Night Watch. A four-foot tall, pigeon-chested, bandy-legged man, with the muscle tone of an elastic band and a certain resemblance to a chimpanzee. The only reason you can't say that Nobby is close to the animal kingdom is that the animal kingdom would move further away. Nobby is actually smaller than many dwarfs (er . . . we compromised a bit on this!).

He is rumoured to have terrible personal habits, although these appear to be no more than a penchant for petty theft (usually from people too unconcious or, for preference, too dead to argue) an ability to do tricks with his facial boils, and a liking for folk dancing.

Men like Nobby can be found in any armed force. Although their grasp of the minutiae of the regulations is usually encyclopaedic, they take good care never to be promoted beyond, perhaps, corporal. He smokes incessantly, but the weird thing is that any cigarette smoked by Nobby becomes a dog-end almost instantly but remains a dog-end indefinitely or until lodged behind his ear, which is a sort of nicotine Elephants' Graveyard.

Nobby is known to have served as a quartermaster in the army of the Duke of Pseudopolis. There are rumours that he had to join the Watch after items missing from the stores were found in his kit. Since the items were the entirety of the store inventory, Nobby's kit at the time consisted of two warehouses.

Lord Vetinari

First name Havelock. Age uncertain. Background unavailable. Reputedly trained at the Assassins' Guild school. Now supreme ruler of the city of Ankh-Morpork, to which he is totally devoted. Tall, thin, and generally to be seen wearing black.

He appears to have survived by being equally distrusted and disliked by all interest groups in the city but also by carefully not being as unpopular as every interest group is to all the others.

Technically, Vetinari seems to have given in to every demand of every Guild for years, so the Guilds are driving themselves mad wondering why he is therefore still in charge. His genius lies in the realisation that everyone craves stability even more than they hunger after justice or truth. This policy is dimly perceived by the more intelligent Guild leaders in the city. <u>Annoying as the Patrician is, however, it is so easy to think of someone worse.</u>

He is entirely without vices in any normal sense of the word. If he had any, we can be sure some Guild or other would have made use of them by now. It is true that he has banned street theatre and hangs mime artists upside down in a scorpion pit opposite a sign which says 'Learn The Words', but this may be considered an excusable peccadillo or possibly an amusing character trait. He does have a small and very old terrier, called Wuffles, to which he is said to be quite attached.

Lord Vetinari lives in what was once the royal family's Winter Palace in Morpork. He manages the city either from a wooden seat at the foot of the steps on which is the ancient golden throne of the city, or more usually from the Oblong Office, high in the palace. This is where he gathers information. People tell him things, for all sort of reasons. He has a bedroom. He presumably sleeps.

Lady Ramkin

Sybil Deirdre Olgivanna. The Ramkin Family Motto is: NON SUMET NULLUS PRO RESPONSO (Never Take No For An Answer).

Lady Ramkin is the richest woman in Ankh-Morpork.

She is a toweringly big lady, with a mass of chestnut hair (a wig – no-one who has much to do with dragons keeps their own hair for long). The Ramkins have never bred for beauty, they've bred for healthy solidity and big bones, and Lady Sybil is the shining result.

For almost all of her life she has apparently confined her own personal breeding to swamp dragons, which she keeps in pens behind the house, and she is the tower of strength behind the Sunshine Sanctuary for Sick Dragons. For dragon handling, she wears huge and fearsomely padded armour. She is the author of several self-published volumes on the diseases of the dragon, which is a fruitful and probably endless field of study.

Costumes

We played most of the characters around the Georgian period, although the City Watch were attired in uniforms of the English Civil War period, which helped to point up the anachronism that they are viewed as by their citizens.

The clowns we dressed in the traditional gear – huge tailcoats, baggy trousers, tiny hats, fluorescent curly wigs, etc. Dr Whiteface, however, was dressed more severely in a white, Commedia del Arte, clown costume.

Our Patrician wore a long, voluminous black robe over a high necked 'Russian peasant' black shirt, black trousers and boots. On his head he wore a black skull cap. The effect was one of power combined with ecclesiastical austerity.

Scenery

Virtually none. We had our gargoyle mounted on the centre of the back wall of our stage, on our on-stage gallery, throughout. Other than that, we used the minimum of furniture necessary to establish the settings (a multi-purpose table and chairs, a cut-out Victorian bath for Vimes, a bed (easily stowable).

Special Effects

Other little bits and pieces included:

The Gonne

We made this ourselves – wooden stock, plastic tubing barrel painted with Hammerite, shoulder strap from a sports bag. The whole thing based very much on the picture by Josh Kirby on the cover of the hardback book, which I knew was how Terry imagined the gonne to look. Because it could not itself fire, whenever it had to be discharged on stage, the actor had concealed about his person a small starting pistol with loud blanks, so that he could fire *that* whenever the gonne was supposed to discharge itself.

The Gargoyle

Well, OK, he's not essential, but we thought he was a bit of fun and that it would have been a pity to cut him out. We had him built for us by Spyder's FX and he had eyes that could look left and right as he talked.

Detritus

Again, we had him made by Spyder's FX. Basically, he was a very effective head mask and gloves, worn with a knitted chainmail outfit, breast- and back-plate, hired from a local firm.

The Pork Futures Warehouse

Simply, we flooded the stage with cold blue light. If you can run to it, then a bit of stage smoke, or dry ice, would also be nice (yes, I know that dry ice, unlike the contents of the futures warehouse, is a real pig to handle but it does give a good effect!).

The Sewers

Again, a simple lighting effect – a rippling water effect on a bare stage otherwise lit with gungy green lamps, supplemented by a sound FX tape of dripping water. Surprisingly effective – and no set to change.

The Librarian

We didn't include him in our version, but if you have someone who's desperate to lose weight, you might like to know that the Orangutan Foundation do now have an orang-utan costume that they may be prepared to loan to a careful user – subject to its being returned in at least as good a condition as that in which it went out, and to a donation for their organisation. They can be contacted via Ashley Leiman, Orangutan Foundation, 7 Kent Terrace, London, NW1 4RP (Tel/Fax: 0171 724 2912).

The Music

We try to choose incidental music which complements the show. Here, the werewolf theme meant that we could underline for the audience the changes that Angua is undergoing off-stage by selecting incidental music which, initially, references itself to *American Werewolf in London* – *Bad Moon Rising* (Credence Clearwater Revival), *Blue Moon* (the Marcels) and so on. Careful choices can add to your play an additional dimension of humour, not available to the books, which reflects Terry's own propensity to make subtle, passing, references to literature, films, plays and so on.

Stephen Briggs
May 1997

TERRY PRATCHETT'S
MEN AT ARMS

adapted for the stage by Stephen Briggs

CAST OF CHARACTERS

Edward d'Eath: *an assassin*
Samuel Vimes: *Captain, City Watch*
Havelock Vetinari: *the Patrician*
Frederick Colon: *Sergeant, City Watch* ·
Cuddy: *Dwarf Lance-Constable, City Watch*
Detritus: *Troll Lance-Constable, City Watch*
'Nobby' Nobbs: *Corporal, City Watch*
Carrot Ironfoundersson: *Corporal, City Watch*
Angua: *W... Lance-Constable, City Watch*
Beano: *a Clown*
Death: *an anthropomorphic personification*
Morecombe: *solicitor & vampire*
Lady Sybil Ramkin: *a noblewoman*
Bjorn Hammerhock: *a dwarf artificer*
Downey: *an assassin*
Dr Cruces: *Head Assassin*
Drumknott: *Patrician's secretary*
Selachi: *a noble*
Rust: *a noble*
Skater: *a noble*
'Mayonnaise' Quirke: *Captain, City Day Watch*
Willikins: *Ramkin family servant*
Boffo: *a clown*
Dr Whiteface: *Head Clown*
Cornice-Overlooking-Broadway: *a gargoyle (possibly off-stage voice)*
Footnote: *a footnote*
Leonard Da Quirm: *an inventor*
Voice of the Gonne: *(off-stage only)* ·
The Werewolf: *(non-speaking)*
Footnote #2: *another, older, footnote*

Play first performed by the Studio Theatre Club
on 15 to 19 November 1994
at the Unicorn Theatre, Abingdon.

SCENE 1 – BARE STAGE

On stage, in the dark, are Carrot, Vimes, the Patrician and Edward d'Eath. Klaxon. The Footnote enters in a follow-spot.

FOOTNOTE

Hello. Welcome to Ankh-Morpork – the oldest existing city on the Discworld. Ankh-Morpork: as loud as a curse in a cathedral, as colourful as a bruise and as full of industry, activity and general business as a dead dog on a termite mound. Ankh-Morpork is where people go to make huge wads of money while not being killed on an official basis.

Last year Ankh-Morpork's City Watch, who would make the Keystone Cops look like The Sweeney, saved the city from a sixty-foot, fire-breathing dragon. But now a new terror threatens.

And these . . .

(*Tight spots come up, dimly, on the four principals*)

. . . are your principal characters:

(*She walks over to the Patrician. His spot comes up full*)

Lord Vetinari. Patrician of Ankh-Morpork. The city no longer has kings, after a bit of civil unpleasantness hundreds of years ago, involving an axe.

3

Ruling this city is like juggling chainsaws on a tightrope. He is so very good at it that Machiavelli would describe him as being 'a bloody cunning bastard and no mistake'.

Lord Vetinari, despite being a . . .

(*Lord Vetinari turns to look speculatively at Footnote, who emphasises the next word*)

. . . a BENEVOLENT dictator, is in fact the ultimate democrat. He believes in the principle of one man, one vote. However, he believes even more emphatically that the man with the vote should be him.

He is entirely without vices in any normal sense of the word. If he had any, we can be sure someone would have made use of them by now.

His only known peccadillo is a tendency to have common actors put to death without trial or mercy.

(*With no change of expression, the other players take one sideways step further away from the Patrician*)

Strangely, the person with whom he gets on best – or least badly – is Corporal Carrot Ironfoundersson of the Watch. They share the same obsessive interest in, one might almost say love of, the city itself.

(*She walks over to Carrot. The Patrician's spot dims; Carrot's comes up full*)

Corporal Carrot Ironfoundersson. A dwarf (by adoption). His adoptive dwarf parents found him in the woods as a toddler, wandering near the bodies of his real parents, who had been victims of a bandit attack. Also in the wreckage of the cart was a sword, and a ring which was very similar to one recorded as having once been a part of the royal jewellery of Ankh.

His adoptive parents, embarrassed at his size, arranged for him to join the Night Watch in Ankh-Morpork because, they had been told, it would make a man of him. Like all dwarfs, when away from home he writes at least once a week, in letters full of optional spelling and punctuation as erratic as acne.

He's honest, decent, truthful and brave. Let's face it, he's the rightful heir to the throne.

(*Carrot's chest swells*)

It's written all over him . . . and people are beginning to learn to read.

(*She walks over to Vimes. Carrot's spot fades down; Vimes' comes up full*)

Corporal Carrot works for Captain Samuel Vimes. Captain of the Ankh-Morpork City Watch. Badge Number 177. Due to retire to get married, as our play begins. Also decent, in his way – but it is a cynical, despondent way, the way of a knight whose shining armour has been a bit tarnished by twenty years on these mean streets. What would you expect in a city where assassination is legal and thieves are licenced?

5

He loathes the idea of kings, and hates the undead, trolls and Assassins. He hates the city in the same way; it's his to hate. So gods help anyone who threatens it.

(*She crosses to Edward. Vimes' spot down; Edward's spot up*)

And this brings us to Edward d'Eath. Edward believes that Ankh-Morpork should be ruled by a king. He has undertaken extensive research, and has found a wealth of evidence which suggests very strongly that Corporal Carrot is directly descended from the rightful kings of Ankh. Regrettably, Edward's obsession has somewhat turned his mind.

Edward d'Eath was sent to the Assassins' Guild because they had the best school for those whose social rank is higher than their intelligence. If he'd been trained as a Fool, he'd have invented satire and made dangerous jokes about the Patrician. If he'd been trained as a Thief, he'd have broken into the Palace and stolen something very valuable from the Patrician. However, he had been trained as an Assassin . . .

(*Klaxon. Footnote exits. Scene ends*)

SCENE 2 – A ROOM IN THE PATRICIAN'S PALACE

The Patrician and Captain Vimes enter onto an area above the stage, talking.

PATRICIAN
Well, of course, I was very saddened to receive your letter, Captain . . .

VIMES
Yes, sir.

PATRICIAN
And, of course, you'll be quite a rich man, Captain . . .

VIMES
Yes, sir.

PATRICIAN
But of course, I quite understand. The Ramkin country estates are very extensive, and I am sure that Lady Ramkin will appreciate your strong right arm.

VIMES
Sir?

PATRICIAN
I hope you have thought about that. You will have new responsibilities.

VIMES
Yes, sir.

PATRICIAN
I seem to be conducting both sides of this conversation, Captain. (*pause*) There is, of course, the matter of your successor. Have you any suggestions, Captain?

VIMES
Well, not Fred Colon . . . He's one of Nature's Sergeants . . .

(*Lights cross-fade to main stage area, where Colon is addressing Cuddy and Detritus*)

COLON
Atten-tion!

(*Detritus springs to attention and cracks off a salute which stuns him, temporarily*)

(*Colon sighs*)

Let's try that once more, shall we Lance-Constable Detritus. I dunno. Just 'cos the Patrician got a letter from the Silicon Anti-Defamation League, he sez we've got to reflect the ethnic makeup, like we was some kind of dressing table mirror. So we 'ave to 'ave a troll in the Watch . . .

Look . . . the trick is, you stops your hand just above your ear. That way, you might manage not to completely demolish your head in your first week.

Now then, Lance-Constable Cuddy . . . Lance-Constable Cuddy?

CUDDY
Here, Sergeant.

COLON
Oh, yes, right. So you are.

CUDDY
I'm taller than I look.

COLON
Oh gods, add 'em up and divide by two and you've got two normal men, except normal men don't join the Guard. A troll and a dwarf. And that ain't the worst of it . . .

(*Lights cross-fade back to the Patrician and Vimes*)

VIMES
Not Colon, then. He's not as young as he was. Time he stayed in the Watch House, catching up on the paper-work. Besides, he's got a lot on his plate.

PATRICIAN
Sergeant Colon has always had a lot on his plate, I should say.

VIMES

With the new recruits, I mean, sir. That you, er, asked me to have. You remember, sir? No room in the Day Watch, or the Palace Guard, so why don't I include some ethnic minorities in the Night Watch. Sir.

PATRICIAN

How about Corporal Nobbs?

(*Lights come up on Nobbs, leaning against a wall and cleaning his teeth with a bit of grubby wood – or better still, smoking a fag, 'squaddie-style', while scratching his bum with his other hand*)

PATRICIAN & VIMES

No.

(*Lights out on Nobby*)

PATRICIAN

And then, of course, there is Corporal Carrot. A fine young man. Already making a name for himself, I gather.

VIMES

That's . . . true.

PATRICIAN

A further promotion opportunity, perhaps? I would value your advice.

(*Lights cross-fade to the main stage area. Carrot and Angua enter DSL*)

CARROT

This is the Hubwards Gate. To the whole city. Which is
what we guard.

ANGUA

What from?

CARROT

Oh, you know. Barbarian hordes, warring tribesmen,
bandit armies . . . that sort of thing.

ANGUA

What? Just us?

CARROT

Us? Oh no! That'd be silly, wouldn't it? No, if you see
anything like that you just ring your bell as hard as you
like.

ANGUA

What happens then?

CARROT

Sergeant Colon and Nobby and the rest of 'em will come
running along just as soon as they can.

ANGUA

R-i-ght. So what do we do now?

CARROT

We proceed back to the Watch House. Sergeant Colon'll
be reading out the evening report likely as not.

ANGUA

Sergeant Colon. He's the tubby bald one, yes? [*Or whatever your Colon looks like!*]

CARROT

That's right.

ANGUA

Why has he got a pet monkey?

CARROT

A pet monkey? Ah. I think it is Corporal Nobbs to whom you refer . . .

ANGUA

Oh. Sorry. And who's the one with the granite face?

CARROT

Ah yes, that's Lance-Constable Detritus. Like you, he's a part of the Patrician's new scheme to recruit more minori—

ANGUA

No, not him. That man. Face like thunder. Always looks disgruntled.

CARROT

Oh, that's Captain Vimes. But he's never been gruntled, I think. He's retiring at the end of the week. He's getting married.

ANGUA

He doesn't look very happy about it. I don't think he likes the new recruits. I shall call him Old Stoneface!

CARROT

Well, don't do it where he can hear – he doesn't like trolls much. We couldn't get a word out of him all day when he heard we had to advertise for a troll recruit. And then we had to have a dwarf, otherwise there'd be trouble. I'm a dwarf, actually . . . but the other dwarfs don't believe it.

ANGUA

You don't say?

CARROT

My mother had me by adoption. I was found in the wreckage of a burned-out cart. This sword was found nearby . . .

(*magical chord*)

ANGUA

Anyway – I'm not a troll, or a dwarf.

CARROT

No, but you are a w—

ANGUA

That's it, is it? Good grief! This is the Century of the Fruitbat, you know. Ye gods, does he really think like that?

CARROT
Yes, but he's retiring in a couple of days. He's a decent man when you get to know him. Just a bit set in his ways.

ANGUA
Set? More like congealed!

(*Lights fade to blackout as they exit*)

SCENE 3 – THE FRONT OFFICE IN THE WATCH HOUSE

On stage are Sergeant Colon, Corporals Carrot and Nobbs, and Lance-Constables Cuddy, Angua and Detritus. Colon stands at a lectern

COLON
Right then, people. Settle down.

NOBBS
We are settled down, Fred.

COLON
That's Sergeant to you, Nobby.

NOBBS
Well, I feels daft, standing around listening to you going on about—

COLON
We got to do it proper, now there's more of us. Right! Ahem. Right. OK. We welcome to the Guard today Lance-Constable Detritus – don't salute! – and Lance-Constable Cuddy, also Lance-Constable Angua. Now then, first thing to watch out for is—

CARROT
Sergeant?

COLON

Yes, Corporal Carrot?

CARROT

Aren't you forgetting something, Sergeant? The recruits? Something they've got to take?

COLON

Well, they've taken all their equipment. All signed for.

CARROT

The oath, Sergeant. They've got to take the oath.

COLON

Oh. Right? What? Well. Er, perhaps you'd like to do the honours, Corporal.

CARROT

Yes sir! Right, recruits! Raise your right hands . . . that's the one nearest to Lance-Constable Angua, Lance-Constable Detritus . . . (*he closes his eyes*)

I comma square bracket recruit's name square bracket comma . . .

RECRUITS

I comma square bracket recruit's name square bracket comma . . .

CARROT

. . . do solemnly swear by bracket recruit's deity of choice square bracket . . .

RECRUITS

. . . do solemnly swear by bracket recruit's deity of choice square bracket . . .

CARROT

. . . to uphold the Laws and Ordinances of the city of Ankh-Morpork comma *'Land of Hope & Glory' plays quietly under this speech* serve the public trust comma and defend the subjects of his stroke her bracket delete whichever is inapplicable bracket Majesty bracket name of reigning monarch bracket without fear comma favour comma or thought of personal safety full stop Gods Save the King stroke Queen bracket delete whichever is inapplicable bracket full stop.

(Pause. He opens his eyes)

COLON

Yes, well, thank you, Corporal Carrot. Now then, you lot, do you all swear to what he just said?

RECRUITS

We do!

NOBBS

Where's Captain Vimes? He should be doing this.

COLON

Captain Vimes is off learning how to be a civilian. Now what's left, Corporal Carrot?

CARROT

They've got to take the King's Shilling, Sergeant.

COLON

Oh yes (*he fishes out three coins*). Right, well, here you all are. This is called the King's Shilling. Dunno why. It's just an ordinary dollar. You gotta have it when you join. Regulations, see. Shows you've joined.

Now then . . . where was I . . . Grabber Hoskins has been let out of jail again, so be on the look out, you know what he's like when he's had a celebratory drink, and bloody Coalface the troll beat up four men last night. And another group of damn rocks, er, sorry, that's fellow citizens of the troll persuasion, have got some kind of march down Short Street. What's that about, then?

DETRITUS

It Troll New Year.

COLON

Is it? Well, I suppose we got to learn about this stuff. And there's this gritsucker, er, dwarf rally or something . . .

CUDDY

Battle of Koom Valley Day. Famous victory over the trolls.

DETRITUS

Yeah. From ambush.

CUDDY
Ambush? It was not—

(*Klaxon. Footnote enters*)

FOOTNOTE
To understand why dwarfs and trolls don't get on, you have to go back a long way. They get along like chalk and cheese. Very like chalk and cheese, in fact – one's organic, the other isn't. Trolls hate dwarfs because they make a living by smashing up rocks with valuable minerals in them and the silicon-based lifeforms called trolls are, basically, rocks with valuable minerals in them.

Dwarfs hate trolls because, after you've just found an interesting seam of valuable minerals, you don't like rocks that suddenly stand up and tear your arm off because you've just stuck a pick-axe in their ear.

(*Klaxon. Footnote exits*)

COLON
Shut up, you two. Look, it says here they're marching up Short Street. Is this right?

CARROT
Trolls going one way, dwarfs going the other?

NOBBS
Now there's a parade you don't want to miss. Dwarfs and trolls get on like a house on fire. Ever been in a burning house, miss?

CARROT
Come on! We've got to do something!

COLON
Right. But remember, let's be careful out there.

NOBBS (*exiting*)
Yeah, let's be careful to stay in here!

(*Lights down as they exit*)

SCENE 4 – A STREET IN ANKH-MORPORK

Beano, a clown enters. He is in full costume and make-up. From the opposite side of the stage enters Edward d'Eath, wearing a black hooded robe.

EDWARD
  Beano.

BEANO
  Oh, hello . . . . it's Edward, isn't it? Edward d'Eath?

  (*No reply*)

  Erm, I was just going back to the Guild.

  (*The hooded figure nods*)

  Are you OK?

EDWARD
  I'm s-sorry about this. But it is for the g-good of the city. It is nothing p-personal.

  (*He strikes Beano over the head with an iron bar. Beano collapses on the floor. Edward looks at where he has fallen, but Beano gets up again*)

BEANO
  Ow, that hurt . . . oh . . . no, it doesn't. (*He notices Edward staring at the ground*) Edward?

EDWARD (*talking to the 'body'*)
Oh no! I didn't mean to hit you that hard! I only wanted you out of the way!

(*Unseen by Edward or Beano, Death enters*)

BEANO
Why'd you have to hit me at all? (*It registers that Edward is not talking to* him) Who are you talking to?

DEATH
KNOCK, KNOCK.

BEANO (*automatic reaction*)
Who's there?

DEATH
DEATH.

BEANO
Death who?

(*a pause*)

DEATH
I WONDER . . . CAN WE START AGAIN? I DON'T SEEM TO HAVE THE HANG OF THIS.

BEANO
Sorry?

EDWARD (*still talking to the 'body'*)
I'm s-orry! I meant it for the best.

22

(He starts to drag the 'body' away)

BEANO
Nothing personal, he says. I'm glad it wasn't anything personal. I should hate to think I've just been killed because it was personal.

DEATH
IT'S JUST THAT IT HAS BEEN SUGGESTED THAT I SHOULD BE MORE OF A PEOPLE PERSON.

BEANO
I mean, why? I thought we were getting on really very well. It's very hard to make friends in my job. In your job, too, I suppose.

DEATH
BREAK IT TO THEM GENTLY, AS IT WERE.

BEANO
One minute walking along, the next minute dead. Why?

DEATH
THINK OF IT MORE AS BEING . . . DIMENSIONALLY DISADVANTAGED.

BEANO *(turning to him)*
What are you talking about?

DEATH
YOU'RE DEAD.

BEANO
Yes, I know.

DEATH
IF YOU WOULD CARE TO FOLLOW ME . . .

BEANO
Will there be custard pies? Red noses? Juggling? Are there likely to be baggy trousers?

DEATH
NO.

BEANO
I like it.

(*Lights out as scene ends*)

SCENE 5 – THE OFFICE OF MR MORECOMBE, A SOLICITOR

Morecombe is on stage, at his desk. Vimes enters.

MORECOMBE
Ah, Captain Vimes. Thank you for coming. Lady Ramkin should be here shortly.

VIMES
What's this all about?

MORECOMBE
Captain Vimes, I have been the Ramkin family solicitor for many . . . many years. Now that your marriage to her Ladyship is drawing near, she wanted to ensure that the correct financial provision was established. In particular, she wishes control of the Ramkin money to pass to you, as her husband.

VIMES
But I . . .

MORECOMBE
The estate is worth about seven million dollars a year.

VIMES
How much?

MORECOMBE

I believe I am right in saying the estate, including the farms, the areas of urban development and the small area of unreal estate near Unseen University, are together worth approximately seven million dollars a year.

(*Klaxon. Footnote enters*)

FOOTNOTE

Captain Vimes always had trouble with money. He had a theory about how rich people got rich. It was his 'Boots' theory of socio-economic unfairness:

Vimes earned thirty-eight dollars a month. Plus allowances. A really good pair of leather boots cost fifty dollars. But an affordable pair of boots, which were good for a season or two and then leaked like hell when the cardboard gave out, cost about ten dollars.

Those were the kind of boots Vimes always bought, and wore until the soles were so thin he could tell where he was on a foggy night by the feel of the cobbles.

But the thing was that good boots lasted for years and years. A man who could afford fifty dollars for a pair of boots had a pair of boots that'd still be keeping his feet dry in ten years' time, while a poor man who could only afford cheap boots would have spent a hundred dollars in the same time – and would still have wet feet.

(*Klaxon. Footnote exits*)

VIMES

It's all mine?

MORECOMBE
From the hour of your wedding to Lady Sybil. Although she has instructed me that you are to have access to all her accounts as of the present moment. Here.

(*He hands Vimes a letter*)

VIMES
But . . . we'll own them together . . .

MORECOMBE
Lady Sybil is very specific. She is deeding all the property to you as her husband. She has a somewhat . . . old-fashioned approach.

Should you predecease her, of course, it will revert to her by common right of marriage. Or to any fruit of the union, of course.

VIMES
What? Fruit of . . . ?

MORECOMBE
Lady Sybil, while not as young as she was, is a fine woman, and there is no reason why—

[*Town clock bell FX here: extended cacophony of chimes to establish that time in Ankh-Morpork varies upon which clock you take notice of. This effect occurs again later in the play and again at the end in the 'confrontation' scene.*]

(*Lady Ramkin enters*)

LADY RAMKIN
Hello, Morecombe, you old vampire!

VIMES
My La . . . er . . . Sybil – what's all this? I really can't—

LADY RAMKIN
Did you go and see Havelock?

VIMES
Who?

LADY RAMKIN
Havelock Vetinari. The Patrician.

VIMES
The Patrician? Havelock? Erm, yes. Yes, I did.

LADY RAMKIN
Good. And you hadn't forgotten about the Dinner tomorrow night, had you. It's time you met the Right People. We shall expect you up at the house at eight o'clock. And don't look like that, you'll enjoy it. You're far too good a man to spend his nights traipsing around dark wet streets. It's time you got on in the world.

VIMES
But I like . . . well, no, I don't actually like . . . but—

LADY RAMKIN
Have you got a hanky?

VIMES
   What? Oh, er . . .

   (*He fishes out a grubby example*)

LADY RAMKIN
   Spit.

   (*Vimes looks about to expectorate on Morecombe's floor*)

On the hanky.

   (*Vimes spits on the hanky. She wipes away a smudge on his forehead*)

There we are. That's better. Now then, you go off and keep the streets safe for us all. Oh, and keep your eyes peeled for a loose swamp dragon, would you? One seems to have escaped, or been pinched. Answers to the name of Chubby. Off you go then!

VIMES
   Er, right!

   (*He exits as the lights black out*)

SCENE 6 – A BALCONY OVERLOOKING SHORT STREET, ANKH-MORPORK

(On stage are Colon, Cuddy, Detritus and Nobbs. They are peering down. We can hear FX of a large crowd)

NOBBS

Don't see why we can't let 'em fight it out amongst themselves and then arrest the losers. That's what we always used to do.

COLON
The Patrician gets really shirty about ethnic trouble. He gets really sarcastic about it. I don't fancy being the one that has to tell him there's been an all-out battle on Short Street between trolls celebrating their New Year and dwarfs celebrating Battle of Koom day. Do you?

(Carrot and Angua enter)

CARROT
What're we going to do, Sarge?

COLON
Well, er . . . (*a thought*) Corporal Carrot?

CARROT
Sarge?

COLON
Just nip down there and sort this lot out, will you?

CARROT
Right you are, Sergeant. Lance-Constables Cuddy and Detritus – don't salute! – come with me.

(*They exit*)

ANGUA
You can't let him go down there. It's certain death!

NOBBS
Got a real sense of duty, that boy.

COLON
Don't worry, miss – he—

ANGUA
Lance-Constable.

COLON
What?

ANGUA
Lance-Constable. Not miss. Carrot says I don't have any sex while I'm on duty.

(*Colon 'harrumphs' embarrassedly. Nobby has a brief coughing fit*)

COLON
What I mean is – Lance-Constable – young Carrot's got bags of krisma.

ANGUA
    Krisma?

COLON
    Bags of it.

(*Lights cross-fade to the stage area. Carrot stands, with
Cuddy and Detritus behind him. 'Ahead' of him, to his
stage left and right, and out of the fourth wall, are two
vast armies of dwarfs and trolls, regrettably too vast to
even think of getting into our little theatre, but if you've
got them, by all means put them on your stage!*)

CARROT
    (*Looking left*)

Morning, Mr Bauxite! Morning Mr Igneous! Hope the
leg's better!

    (*Looking right, and slightly down*)

Morning Mr Cumblethigh! Mr Stronginthearm! Mrs
Stronginthearm!

    (*To all*)

If you could all just stop and listen to me . . .

    (*The crowd noise lessens*)

Now then, gentlemen . . .

CUDDY (*sotto voce, behind Carrot*)
    Hah! It was too an ambush! And your mother was an ore!

CARROT

. . . and ladies. I'm sure there's no need for this belligerent manner . . .

DETRITUS

You ambush us, too! My great-grandfather he at Koom Valley. He tell me.

CARROT

. . . in our fair city on such a lovely day. I must ask you, as good citizens of Ankh-Morpork . . .

CUDDY

Yeah? You don't even know who your father is!

CARROT

. . . that, while you must certainly celebrate your proud ethnic folkways, to profit by the examples of my fellow officers here, who have sunk their differences . . .

DETRITUS

I smash your head, you roguesome dwarf . . .

CARROT

. . . for the better benefit of . . .

CUDDY

I could take you with one hand tied behind by back!

CARROT

. . . the City, whose badge they are . . .

(It dawns on Carrot that the 'crowd' are not paying attention to him. He turns and sees Cuddy and Detritus about to come to blows. Carrot is livid)

Lance-Constable Detritus! Salute!

(Detritus executes a big salute. The down-stroke smacks Cuddy on the head, knocking him unconscious. The up-stroke, as before, connects with his own head and knocks him, too, senseless to the ground. Carrot now turns on the crowd)

Right! *(to the dwarfs)* You've got weapons, haven't you? Own up! If the dwarfs who've got weapons don't drop them right this minute the entire parade, and I mean the entire parade, will be in very grave trouble. I'm serious about this!

(A loud metallic crash, as of several hundred swords, axes, knives, hitting a cobbled street)

And as for you *(turning to the trolls)* I shall definitely be patrolling around Quarry Lane tonight and I won't be seeing any trouble. Will I? Will I?

(Mumble of a crowd all reluctantly saying 'Yes, Corporal Carrot')

Right. Now off you go. And let's have no more of this nonsense, there's good chaps.

(Lights come up on the balcony again)

ANGUA
I really thought he was going to die.

NOBBS
Funny that. If we was to try it, we'd be little bits of mince. But it seems to work for him.

COLON
Krisma.

ANGUA
Do you mean charisma?

COLON
Yeah, one of them things . . .

NOBBS
I suppose, he's just an easy lad to like. (*an explosion*) Blimey! That sounded like it came from the Assassins' Guild!

COLON
Oh dear. Come on, then, we'd better look into it.

(*They exit. A robed figure crosses the stage, carrying the gonne wrapped in a cloth. Centre stage, the figure pauses and partly unwraps the package*)

VOICE OF THE GONNE (*over the speakers*)
Now – you're mine!

(*The figure furtively wraps the gonne, and exits as the lights black out*)

SCENE 7 – THE ASSASSINS' GUILD, FILIGREE STREET

One area of the stage is visible as the entrance to the Guild museum. There are fragments of broken display case on the ground, and a little smoke drifts around. Vimes, Carrot, Detritus, Angua, Colon, Cuddy and Nobbs are on stage. An assassin, Downey, enters.

NOBBS
Blimey – I never thought I'd ever see the inside of the Assassins' Guild.

(Klaxon – the Footnote enters)

FOOTNOTE
The Assassins' Guild is next to and shares a wall with the Fools' Guild. One is a pleasant, airy building, whose corridors echo with the laughter of students. The other is a gaunt, forbidding edifice, and silent except for the occasional muffled sob and the sad jingle of bells.

One turns out people who admittedly must in the course of their duties sometimes stab, poison or otherwise inhume their patients. But at least they never ask them to believe that pouring whitewash down someone's trousers is funny.

(Klaxon – Footnote exits)

DOWNEY
What are you doing here?

VIMES
Fetch me the Master of Assassins. Now!

DOWNEY
Hah! Your uniform doesn't scare me.

VIMES (*looking down at himself*)
You're right. This is not a scary uniform. I'm sorry. Forward, Corporal Carrot and Lance-Constable Detritus.

Now these, I think you'll agree, are scary uniforms.

DOWNEY
I'll just go and get the Master, shall I?

CARROT
Thank you for your co-operation.

(*Dr Cruces enters*)

DR CRUCES
Don't bother, Downey. I'm here. And what is the meaning of this?

VIMES (*pointedly ignoring Cruces*)
Sergeant Colon, I want you to go back to the Watch House with Nobby and Detritus.

COLON (*saluting smartly*)
  Yes sah!

  (*He, Nobbs and Detritus march off. Vimes turns to Cruces*)

VIMES
  Ah, Dr Cruces.

DR CRUCES
  Who sent for you? What gives you the right to invade Guild property? Walking around as if you own the place?

VIMES (*extracting Morecombe's letter from his breastplate*)
  Well, if you would like the most fundamental reason . . . it is because I rather think I do.

  (*Cruces briefly examines the letter.*)

DR CRUCES
  I see. The freehold, at least.

VIMES
  Quite so. And now, perhaps you'll tell me what's been going on?

DR CRUCES (*His lips move for a while as if he's trying out various excuses*)
  Fireworks. Yes. That's right. Fireworks. Er . . . Founder's day. Unfortunately someone threw away a lighted match which ignited the box. Which was stored against that wall. Dreadful mess. Fireworks. Yes,

indeed. (*he smiles*) My dear Vimes, much as I appreciate your concern—

VIMES

They were being stored here? It seems to be some sort of museum. Guild memorabilia, that sort of thing?

DR CRUCES

Yes, exactly. Odds and ends. You know how they mount up over the years.

VIMES

Oh, well, that seems to be in order. Sorry to have troubled you, Doctor. I hope we've not inconvenienced you in any way?

DR CRUCES

Of course not. Glad to have been able to put your mind at rest. Fireworks. I'm sure I can rely on you to see yourself out, Captain.

VIMES

Yes, Doctor, of course. Oh, I'm sorry . . . mind like a sieve . . . what was it you said was stolen?

CRUCES

I didn't say anything was stolen, Captain.

(*Cruces exits*)

VIMES (*softly, to himself*)

No, you didn't . . . (*normal voice*) Corporal Carrot, what have you observed?

CARROT
Smells to me like a dragon's exploded in here.

(*Klaxon. Footnote enters*)

FOOTNOTE
Sorry – back again! The swamp dragon's digestive system is very unstable.

Their internal plumbing can re-arrange itself to make the best possible use of any raw materials available for flame-making. The drawback to this talent is that swamp dragon is capable of exploding violently if excited, frightened, aroused, surprised or bored.

It is presumed that the explosive capability is a defence mechanism acting for the good of the species as a whole, since it certainly doesn't work for the individual concerned.

(*Klaxon. Exit*)

VIMES
You're right. I smelled dragon, too. That was the explosion we all heard. Looks as though we've found Chubby.

CUDDY
Chubby?

VIMES
Lady Sybil's lost dragon. (*He looks at the broken display case*) And something's been taken. Look, there was a card pinned here – someone's taken that, too. I'd give a month's pay to know what it said on that card. Bloody

assassins. Assassins and licensed thieves! You know, this was a great city once, lad.

CARROT

What, when we had kings, you mean?

VIMES

Kings! Don't talk to me about kings! It's not right, one man with the power of life and death.

CARROT

But the Patrician's a supreme ruler.

VIMES

But he doesn't sit on a throne and he doesn't say you got to do what you're told because he's got a crown. He says you've got to do what you're told or you'll be killed. At least he's honest about it.

CARROT

Even so, with a good man as king—

VIMES (*becoming heated*)

Yes? And then what? Royalty pollutes people's minds, boy. Honest men start bowing and bobbing just because someone's grandad was a bigger murdering bastard than theirs was. Listen! Maybe we had good kings, once! But kings breed other kings! And blood tells, and you end up with a bunch of arrogant, murdering bastards! Chopping off queens' heads and fighting their cousins every five minutes! And worse! We had centuries of that! And then one day about 300 years ago a man said 'No more!' and we rose up and we fought the bloody nobles and we dragged the king off his throne and we dragged him into Sator Square and chopped his bloody head off! Job well done!

CARROT

Gosh! Who was he, then? The man who said 'No more kings'?

VIMES (*embarrassed at his outburst*)

Oh . . . he was the Commander of the City Watch in those days. They called him Old Stoneface.

CARROT

'Old Stoneface'? And what king was that?

VIMES (*distantly*)

Lorenzo the Kind.

CARROT

I've seen his picture in the palace museum. A fat old man. Surrounded by lots of children.

VIMES (*carefully*)

Oh yes. He was very *fond* of children.

CARROT

And that was the end of the kings of Ankh–Morpork?

VIMES

Oh, they say some of the family got away, but I don't know . . . I'll tell you something else, Carrot, I'd hate to see a good man as king. That'd be really terrifying! Some man with a sword dispensing genuine justice? None of us'd be safe. We've all done things we shouldn've . . . well, I know I have, I don't know about you . . .

Never get in the power of a completely good man, Carrot. If there's a bad man looking down his crossbow at you . . . well, you know he'll gloat and boast, because he's got you in his power, and that's what he's really after, and you may have a chance. But if a really good man thinks you deserve to die, he'll turn and kill you without a word . . . hang on, what's this . . .

(*He sees a piece of paper on the ground and picks it up*)

CARROT
What is it, sir?

VIMES
It's a drawing. Looks like a crossbow stock with a tube tied onto it. (*he pockets it*) Come on!

(*They exit. Cruces enters with Downey*)

DR CRUCES
Thank gods they've gone. (*he surveys the room*) I want a roll-call. Has anyone left the Guild?

DOWNEY
No, sir. The guards on the roof say no-one came in or went out, sir.

DR CRUCES
Very well. Now listen carefully. I want the mess cleared up. I want everyone watched. And the Guild building is to be searched from top to bottom. Understand?

DOWNEY
What are we searching for, Dr Cruces?

DR CRUCES
For . . . anything that is hidden. If you find anything . . .
unfamiliar . . . send for me immediately. And don't touch
it.

DOWNEY
No, sir.

DR CRUCES
And no-one is to speak to the wretched Watch about
this. And now . . . I suppose I shall have to go and tell
the Patrician.

DOWNEY
Hard luck, sir.

(*Lights black out. In the darkness, a shot is heard*)

SCENE 7 'A' – BJORN HAMMERHOCK'S WORKSHOP

On stage is Bjorn Hammerhock, in a low-ceilinged room. He is working at a bench. Edward enters, with the gonne.

HAMMERHOCK
Ah, Mr d'Eath. You have brought it?

EDWARD
Yes, Mr Hammerhock. This is it.

HAMMERHOCK
And what is it you want of me?

EDWARD
The . . . er . . . thing has been left unattended for some while and parts of it seem to have stiffened up. I was hoping that you might repair it.

HAMMERHOCK
I see, yes. Fine craftsmanship. Strange device. Looks like a crossbow without the bow!

EDWARD
Er . . . something like that. Can you make it work again?

HAMMERHOCK
If I can find out what it's supposed to do . . . Amazing. I think that this lever moves the tubes along, presenting

45

a new chamber to the, er, firing hole. The trigger mechanism is really just a tinderbox device. The spring . . . here . . . seems to have rusted through.

I'd like to make some sketches of it, too, though.

(*He bends over it and starts to work. There is a bang and the noise of a ricochet. Hammerhock falls to the ground*)

EDWARD
Oh no! Mr Hammerhock! Mr Hammerhock! No! Not another one! What shall I do? Can't leave him here! Ah – throw him in the Ankh!

(*He starts to drag out the corpse as the lights black out. Then, in the dark, we hear . . .*)

HAMMERHOCK (*off*)
That was lucky. Could've been a nasty accident there.

DEATH (*off*)
HELLO.

HAMMERHOCK (*off*)
And who might you be . . . ? Oh. Right. Where's young Edward taking me?

[*Effect – splash, plus nasty muddy gurgling noises*]

Oh dear. And I can't swim, either.

DEATH (*off*)
THIS WILL NOT, OF COURSE, BE A PROBLEM.

HAMMERHOCK (*off*)
  You're a lot shorter than I thought you'd be.

DEATH (*off*)
  THAT IS BECAUSE I AM KNEELING DOWN,
  MR HAMMERHOCK.

HAMMERHOCK (*off*)
  That tube thing killed me!

DEATH (*off*)
  YES.

HAMMERHOCK (*off*)
  I believe in reincarnation, you know.

DEATH (*off*)
  YES. I HAVE YOU DOWN AS BJORN HAMMER-
  HOCK. THAT MEANS YOU'LL BE BJORN
  AGAIN.

  (*pause*)

  THAT'S A JOKE.

HAMMERHOCK (*off*)
  Oh. Yes. Sorry.

DEATH (*off*)
  I'VE BEEN TOLD THAT I SHOULD TRY TO
  MAKE THE OCCASION A LITLE MORE
  ENJOYABLE.

HAMMERHOCK (*off*)
Bjorn again?

DEATH (*off*)
YES.

HAMMERHOCK (*off*)
I'll think about it.

DEATH (*off*)
THANK YOU. THIS WAY, IF YOU PLEASE.

SCENE 8 – THE OBLONG OFFICE IN THE PATRICIAN'S PALACE

On stage is a chair and a small podium with a book on it. The Patrician's PPS, Drumknott, enters. He is followed by a somewhat apprehensive-looking Dr Cruces.

DRUMKNOTT
If you'd wait here, Dr Cruces. The Patrician said to say he'll be here 'momentarily'.

(*And he sidles out*)

DR CRUCES
You mean he knew I was . . . ? Oh.

(*A pause. He looks around the room. He thinks about sitting then thinks better of it and crosses to the small podium. He picks up the book*)

'Lace-Making for Beginners'.

(*The Patrician glides in*)

PATRICIAN
Ah, Cruces.

DR CRUCES
Aah! (*he drops the book*) Oh, sorry.

49

PATRICIAN
Don't panic, Cruces. I'm not going to eat you. That was
more to the taste of the city's last ruler, I think.

How did it come to be stolen, Doctor?

DR CRUCES
What? Oh, you know. Erm, I can assure you my Lord
that—

PATRICIAN
I'm sure you can. I'm sure you can. There is one
question that intrigues me, however.

DR CRUCES
My Lord?

PATRICIAN
Why was it in the Guild House to *be* stolen? I had been
given to understand it had been destroyed. I'm quite
certain I gave orders.

DR CRUCES
Ah. Er. We – that is my predecessor – thought it should
serve as a warning and an example.

PATRICIAN
Capital! I have always had a great belief in the effective-
ness of examples. So I am sure that you will be able to
sort this out with minimum inconvenience all round.

DR CRUCES
Certainly, my Lord, but—

(*The city's clocks start to strike the quarter. Drumknott enters*)

DRUMKNOTT
Captain Vimes is here to see you, my Lord.

PATRICIAN
Tell him to wait, would you. (*to Cruces, as Drumknott exits*) You were saying?

DR CRUCES
Yes, Captain Vimes. He's taking an interest.

PATRICIAN
Dear me. But that is his job.

DR CRUCES
I must demand that you call him off!

PATRICIAN
Demand?

DR CRUCES
Er, er . . . I mean, erm, he is a servant, after all. I see no reason why he should involve himself in affairs that don't concern him.

PATRICIAN
I rather believe he thinks he's a servant of the law.

DR CRUCES
He's a jack-in-office and an insolent upstart!

PATRICIAN

Dear me. I did not appreciate your strength of feeling. But since you 'demand' it, I will bring him to heel without delay.

DR CRUCES

Thank you.

PATRICIAN

Don't mention it. Do not let me detain you. People always hate it so when I have to detain them. And tell Drumknott to send in the Captain.

(Dr Cruces exits. After a brief pause, Vimes enters)

PATRICIAN

Ah, Vimes. And what is it that brings you here?

VIMES

Someone has killed Mr Hammerhock, sir. A big man in the dwarf community. He's been . . . shot with something. Some kind of siege weapon or something, and dumped in the river. I was just on the way to tell his wife. And then I thought, as I was passing . . .

PATRICIAN

This is very unfortunate.

VIMES

Certainly it was for Mr Hammerhock.

PATRICIAN

Tell me. How did you say he was killed?

VIMES

I don't know. I've never seen anything like it . . . there was just a great big hole. But I'm going to find out what it was.

PATRICIAN

Hmm. You saw Dr Cruces?

VIMES

Yes, sir.

PATRICIAN

I think you upset him.

VIMES

Sir?

PATRICIAN

Captain Vimes . . .

VIMES

Sir?

PATRICIAN

I know that you are retiring the day after tomorrow and feel, therefore, a little . . . restless. But while you are captain of the Night Watch I am asking you to obey two very specific instructions . . .

VIMES

Sir?

PATRICIAN
You will cease any investigations connected with this theft from the Assassins' Guild. Do you understand? That is entirely Guild business.

VIMES (*keeping his face carefully immobile*)
Sir.

PATRICIAN
I'm choosing to believe that the unspoken word in that sentence was a yes, Captain.

VIMES
Sir.

PATRICIAN
And that one, too. As for the matter of the unfortunate Mr Hammerhock . . . The body was discovered just a short while ago?

VIMES
Yes, sir.

PATRICIAN
Then it's out of your jurisdiction, Captain.

VIMES
What? Sir?

PATRICIAN
The Day Watch can deal with it.

VIMES

But we've never bothered with that hours-of-daylight jurisdiction stuff!

PATRICIAN

Nevertheless, in the current circumstances I shall instruct Captain Quirke to take over the investigation, if it turns out that one is necessary.

VIMES

If . . . ? People don't end up with half their chest gone by accident! Meteor strike, I suppose? Mayonnaise Quirke couldn't find his arse with an atlas! And he's got no idea how to talk to dwarfs! He calls them gritsuckers! It's my jurisdiction!

(*He becomes acutely aware of the impropriety of his manner*)

PATRICIAN

Night Watch. That's what you are, Captain.

VIMES

It's dwarfs we're talking about! If we don't get it right, they'll take the law into their own hands!

PATRICIAN

I've given you an order, Captain.

VIMES

But—

PATRICIAN
You may go.

VIMES
You can't—

PATRICIAN
I said you may go, Captain Vimes!

VIMES
Sir!

(*He salutes, turns and marches out. As he gets to the door post, he thumps it heavily. The Patrician smiles. Drumknott enters*)

DRUMKNOTT
I heard Captain Vimes leave, my Lord. I think we may have to replace part of the woodwork this time.

PATRICIAN
A small price, Drumknott. I think my orders will have the desired effect. Vimes will do practically anything to spite me. I hope.

(*Lights black out*)

SCENE 9 – NEAR ELM STREET

Carrot and Angua stroll on.

ANGUA
It's good of you to see me back to my lodgings.

(*The lights turn to a gloomy exterior. We are aware of a full moon [spot]*)

CARROT
It's no trouble.

ANGUA
But it's out of your way . . .

CARROT
That's all right, I like walking.

(*They stroll*)

ANGUA
Why did you join the Watch?

CARROT
My father said it would make a man of me.

ANGUA
It seems to have worked.

CARROT
Yes, it's the best job there is. Do you know what 'police-man' means?

ANGUA
No.

(*The lights darken to nightfall. The moon comes up*)

CARROT
It means 'man of the polis'. 'Man of the City' . . . OW!

(*He looks at the bottom of his boot*)

Something stuck in my boot.

(*He prises it off*)

ANGUA
What is it?

CARROT
Bit of card.

(*He holds it out. Angua takes it*)

ANGUA
There's something written on it. 'G – O – N – N– E' – Gonne. What does that mean? Mr Gonne's visiting card?

CARROT
No. I think this is important. The Captain ought to know. I'm going to tell him.

ANGUA

Well, here we are. I'm lodging just down there.

CARROT

Elm Street? Not Mrs Cake's?

ANGUA

Yes. Why not?

CARROT

Well . . . I mean, I've got nothing against Mrs Cake, but she . . . well, you know . . . she's not very choosy. You must have noticed? You know, the other guests? Like Reg Shoe.

ANGUA

Oh, you mean the zombie.

CARROT

Er, yes. And Mrs Drull the Flesh–Eating Ghoul.

ANGUA

Oh, she's retired now. She does children's party catering.

CARROT

But they're not . . . really . . . our kind of people, are they? Don't get me wrong. I mean . . . dwarfs? Some of my best friends are dwarfs – my parents are dwarfs. Trolls? No problem at all. Salt of the earth. Literally. But . . . the undead . . . I just wish they go back to where they came from, that's all.

59

ANGUA
Most of them come from around here.

CARROT
I just don't like them. Sorry. I mean, look up there . . . full moon. Know what that means? Place'll be full of wretched werewolves before you can turn around, peeing on the lampposts and wondering how to find their trousers when they turn back.

ANGUA (*coldly*)
I've got to go.

CARROT
Can I see you again?

ANGUA
Tomorrow. At work, I expect. (*more urgently*) I've got to go!

CARROT
OK, OK, tomorrow, then.

(*He exits*)

ANGUA
At last.

(*She glances up at the moon, then runs off stage. Almost immediately there is a wolf howl. A werewolf runs on from the exit Angua used and lopes across the darkened stage.*

[*NOTE – we used a strobe when the werewolf was on . . . mainly to disguise the comparatively ropey wolf costume!*] *Lights black out*)

SCENE 10 – LADY RAMKIN'S HOUSE, SCOONE AVENUE

On stage are Skater, Selachi, Rust, Cruces and Whiteface, plus Lady Ramkin and a servant. There is a buzz of conversation, and laughter.

SKATER (*speaking as the lights go up*)
So I said, I don't care if *it is* the Battle of Koom Day, get those gritsuckers out from underneath my carriage!

(*Skater laughs vacuously, joined by the others. Lady Ramkin smiles in a strained way*)

I mean – they were frightening the horses!

(*They laugh as before. Vimes enters. He looks a tad squiffy. The laughs die and are replaced by an embarrassed pause. Lady Ramkin crosses to him*)

LADY RAMKIN (*sotto*)
Samuel Vimes! You're late! (*she sniffs*) And you haven't changed! And you're drunk!

VIMES
Not yet! But I hope to be!

(*He grabs a glass from the servant's tray*)

SELACHI (*returning to the conversation*)
As I was saying, this unrest is all Vetinari's fault. I mean, we have a city where grocers have as much influence as barons. He even let the Plumbers form a Guild!

RUST
I admit the old kings were not necessarily our kind of people, towards the end. But at least they stood for something. We had a decent city then . . . not letting in all this riff-raff. Isn't that so, Captain?

VIMES
Hmmm?

RUST
The current ethnic problem. Look at Quarry Lane. There's fighting there every night. And those trolls have absolutely no concept of religion.

VIMES (*with an edge to his voice*)
Oh, absolutely. In my view the godless bastards should be rounded up at spearpoint and herded out of the city. And have you noticed how massive their heads are? All rock. Very small brains.

LADY RAMKIN (*aside, to a servant*)
Er, I don't think Captain Vimes wants any more to drink.

(*The front door bell rings*)

VIMES (*cheerfully*)
Wrong!

(He grabs another drink as the servant exits to answer the door)

And what about dwarfs?

SKATER
Notice how small their heads are? Very limited cranial capacity.

RUST
Cunning little devils, too. Sharp as needles.

VIMES
You know, that's what's so damned annoying, isn't it? The way they can be so incapable of any rational thought and so bloody shrewd at the same time.

(The servant enters)

SERVANT
Corporal Carrot, m'lady.

(Carrot enters and crosses to Lady Ramkin)

CARROT
I'm sorry to interrupt, m'lady. I need to see the Captain, I'm afraid.

LADY RAMKIN
Well, we'll leave you to it, Corporal. Come along everyone, let's move into the Library. Rupert, you can play the piano for us. *(they all exit, except Cruces, who lingers by the doorway. She draws Vimes to one side)* What were

you doing? You were trying to make my guests look foolish.

VIMES
No, they were doing that themselves.

LADY RAMKIN
I admit they are a little . . . intolerant. But I've heard you being rude about trolls and dwarfs, too.

VIMES
I've got a right. I know dwarfs and trolls. They hate me, I hate them. Everyone's equal. Everyone's happy. But that lot wouldn't know a troll if it walked over them.

LADY RAMKIN
Maybe you're right. Look, you speak with Corporal Carrot – I'll deal with our guests!

(*She starts to exit*)

Dr Cruces, come along. Have you brought your ocarina?

(*She ushers him out. Vimes crosses to Carrot*)

VIMES
What is it?

CARROT
It's this, sir.

(*He gives the card to Vimes*)

I think it's the label off the thing that used to be in the glass case in the Assassins' Guild.

VIMES

'Gonne'. But what does it mean? Tells us nothing, does it? What was it? Who did it? I mean – a man'd have to be a fool to break into the Assassins' Guild.

CARROT

Yes, sir.

VIMES

Look, these events are all linked. An explosion and a robbery at the Assassins' Guild. Then something puts a bloody great hole in the chest of a dwarf craftsman . . . What did you find in his workshop?

CARROT

Smell of fireworks. Small hole in one of the walls . . .

VIMES

Could've happened any time?

CARROT

No, because there was plaster dust under it, and a dwarf always keeps his workshop spotless. Lots of mechanisms about, though, Mr Hammerhock was very good with his hands. Could never resist a mechanical challenge, sir. Also . . . this was in the hole.

(He hands over a thick lead disc)

VIMES

Looks like a sort of flattened out piece of metal.

(*Cuddy runs in*)

CUDDY

Captain! Captain! It's horrible, sir!

VIMES

What is it, Cuddy?

CUDDY

Another body, sir. In the Ankh, sir. It's a clown. His name was Beano, sir.

VIMES

What the hell's going on? Leave it to Quirke? Not bloody likely! Carrot, get Nobby and Fred Colon to get round to the Fools' Guild! We're going to sort this out!

(*They exit as the lights black out*)

SCENE 11 – THE FOOLS' GUILD, GOD STREET

The stage is empty. The Fools' Guild door has a doorknocker made from a pair of plastic boobs. Nobbs and Colon enter.

NOBBS
Here we are, Sarge – the Fools' Guild. That's where Beano lived.

COLON
Hold it, Nobby. I've been here before. Let me do the door.

> (*He walks up to the door and, at arms' stretch, knocks. There is a short pause and then water squirts out of the plastic boobs' doorknocker*)

See? (*he knocks again*) Come on! No-one's laughing!

> (*To Nobby*)

Sad, isn't it?

BOFFO
I say, I say, I say. Why did the fat man knock at the door?

COLON (*automatically*)
I don't know, why did the fat man knock at the door?

BOFFO
That's what I asked you.

COLON (*grabbing Boffo by the lapels*)
Sergeant Colon. Night Watch. And this is Corporal Nobbs. We're here to ask some questions about the clown that was found corpus derelicti in the river.

BOFFO
Oh, yes. Poor Brother Beano. Erm, it's a long shot, I know, but I don't suppose either of you gentlemen would like to sniff my buttonhole?

COLON
No.

NOBBS
No.

BOFFO
No. I suppose not. It's very difficult, being a clown, you know. I can never remember: is it crying on the outside and laughing on the inside? Or the other way around? (*he sighs*) We've just been holding his funeral. Er, my name's Boffo, by the way. (*he extends a hand to Nobbs*)

COLON
Don't shake it.

BOFFO
Oh. (*he sighs*) It's very sad. No-one would want to kill young Beano. He was a friendly soul. Friends everywhere.

COLON
Almost everywhere.

BOFFO
All I know is, that when I saw him yesterday he looked very . . . odd. I called out to him when he was going through the gates and—

COLON
How do you mean, odd?

BOFFO
Dunno. Not quite himself.

COLON
This was yesterday?

BOFFO
Oh yes. In the morning. I know because—

COLON
Yesterday?

BOFFO
Yes. I remember we were all a bit nervous after the bang next door, when . . .

(*Dr Whiteface enters*)

DR WHITEFACE
Brother Boffo! Who are these gentlemen?

BOFFO

Er . . .

COLON

Night Watch, sir. Investigating our enquiries as to the
fatally deadly lethal demise of the clown Beano, sir.

DR WHITEFACE

This is Guild business, I'm sure we don't need to trouble
the Watch. Do we? Brother Boffo . . . you can report to
my office.

(*He exits*)

NOBBS

What'll he do to you?

BOFFO (*with a sigh*)

Hat full of whitewash, probably. Pie inna face if I'm
lucky. (*new thought*) Well, bye then. Do your best. A lot
of us aren't happy about this. There's quite a few want
to go round and sort out the Assassins.

COLON

Why the Assassins? Why would they want to kill a
clown?

BOFFO

You find his nose. His poor nose. You just find it.

COLON

What? You mean a false one, like yours?

71

BOFFO
False nose? How dare you!

(*And he exits*)

COLON
Did exhibit A have a nose, Nobby?

NOBBS
Yes, Fred. I mean, it's something you notice if it's gone.

COLON
What did he mean, then?

NOBBY
Dunno.

COLON
Me neither. Well, all clowns are crazy, you'd have to be to be funny for a living. Anyway. Look – you seen lots of corpses, yeah? You've ministered to the fallen?

NOBBS
Well, it's a shame to let good boots go to waste.

COLON
So you've noticed how dead bodies get . . . deader. You know, more corpsey.

NOBBS
Going stiff and purple like?

COLON
  Right.

NOBBS
  And then all manky and runny . . .

COLON
  Yes, all right.

NOBBS
  Makes it easier to get the boots off, mind—

COLON
  The point is, Nobby – how old was the clown's corpse
  when we saw it, would you say?

NOBBS
  Couple of days. You can tell because there's this . . .

COLON
  So how come Boffo saw him yesterday morning?

NOBBS
  Bit of a poser, that is.

COLON
  Yeah, well. We'd better tell the Captain. Come on, then.
  Back to the Watch house.

  (*As they exit, the robed figure enters on the balcony, or
  raised area* (*the roof of the Opera House*), *carrying the
  gonne*)

VOICE OF THE GONNE

That damned Watch! That damned Vimes! Exactly the wrong man at the wrong place in history. How can a city run properly with someone like that? Someone like Vimes could upset things. Not because he's clever, eh? A clever watchman's a contradiction in terms. But sheer randomness might cause trouble.

What are you going to do about it?

Kill – him. That's what! There! There he is!

(*Vimes enters onto the stage. With the air of one who is moved by the gonne rather than him moving it, the man takes aim. The lights fade out on him. Almost immediately there are three shots and Vimes ducks*)

VIMES

What the . . . *Oi!* (*the figure runs off*)

(*He turns and looks up at the Opera roof*)

Right! Now I've got you!

(*He runs off. Lights black out. Music link. Vimes appears on the roof, thoroughly out of breath*)

Where the hell are you?

(*He peers over the edge, looking for the shooter. He sees the gargoyle*)

Hello. What's your name, friend?

CORNICE-OVERLOOKING-BROADWAY
'ornice-oggerooking-Oardway.

    (*Klaxon. Enter Footnote*)

FOOTNOTE
Gargoyles are one of Ankh-Morpork's rarer species of
citizen, a type of troll adapted to life on high buildings.
They funnel rainwater into their ears and out through
their mouth, straining out the gnats, pigeons' droppings
and air pollution as valuable nourishment. They also see
most of what goes on although they do, for obvious
reasons, find it hard to talk about it.

    (*Klaxon. Exit Footnote*)

VIMES
Cornice-overlooking-Broadway. Right, Cornice, do you
know who I am?

CORNICE-OVERLOOKING-BROADWAY
Oh. [*ie, 'no'*]

VIMES
I'm Captain Vimes of the Night Watch.

CORNICE-OVERLOOKING-BROADWAY
Ar. Oo erk or Ister Arrot?

VIMES
Do I work for . . . ? You know Mr Carrot?

CORNICE-OVERLOOKING-BROADWAY
Oh, ess. Air-ee-u owes Arrot.

VIMES
Everyone knows him. Yes, I suppose they do. Whereas I've lived in Ankh-Morpork all me life and when I walk down the street everyone says 'Who's that glum bugger?'. Ah well. But you live right up here. How come you know Corporal Carrot?

CORNICE-OVERLOOKING-BROADWAY
Ee cuns uk ere um-imes an awks oo ugg.

VIMES
He comes up here and talks to you? Did someone else come up here? Just now?

CORNICE-OVERLOOKING-BROADWAY
Egg.

VIMES
Did you see who it was?

CORNICE-OVERLOOKING-BROADWAY
Oh. Ee et ogg a ire-erk. I or ing un ah-ay a-ong Or-oh-erns Eet.

VIMES
He let off a firework?

CORNICE-OVERLOOKING-BROADWAY
Egg.

VIMES

And you saw him run away along Holofernes Street?

CORNICE-OVERLOOKING-BROADWAY

Egg. Ee ad a ick. A ire-urk ick.

VIMES

A firework stick? What, like a rocket stick?

CORNICE-OVERLOOKING-BROADWAY

Oh. Ih-ee-ot! A htick – oo oint ik, ik koes ANG!

VIMES

You point it and it goes bang?

CORNICE-OVERLOOKING-BROADWAY

Egg! Oo-id irriot . . .

VIMES

Right. (*he turns to go*) Hello? What's this? (*he stoops to pick it up*) Hmm. Six tubes stuck together. (*he sniffs them*) Fireworks – again. (*pulls out the flattened metal disc and the drawing and looks at it*) Some kind of new weapon. A stick that shoots fire. Whoever it was fired off three shots quicker than you could reload a bow. And I was a good three hundred yards away. Hmm. A new, fast, deadly weapon. The Assassins wouldn't like a weapon like that. Too impersonal. It'd undermine their monopoly on contracted sudden death. They'd want it put away under lock and key . . .

(*Colon, Cuddy and Detritus enter in the dark onto the stage*)

COLON (*still in the dark*)
    Captain! Captain Vimes, sir!

    (*Lights up on stage*)

VIMES
    Colon! Come up here, would you. (*to the gargoyle*) Well,
    thanks, You've been . . . eh-ee elkfhull.

COLON
    Right, sir. You two – wait here!

    (*He exits. Lights out on roof*)

    (*A pause*)

CUDDY
    Look. I just want you to know that I don't like being
    teamed up with you any more than you like being teamed
    up with me.

DETRITUS
    Right.

CUDDY
    But if we're going to have to make the best of it, there'd
    better be some changes, OK?

DETRITUS
    Like what?

CUDDY
    Like it's ridiculous you not even being able to count.

DETRITUS

Can count.

CUDDY

How many fingers am I holding up?

DETRITUS

Two?

CUDDY

Now how many? [3]

DETRITUS

Two . . . plus one more?

CUDDY

Three! Two and one more is three!

DETRITUS

Three. Right. Three.

CUDDY

Good. You can get there.

DETRITUS

I can get there. Two fingers. Two . . . legs. Two . . . arms.
Two . . . ears. (*hold up three fingers*) Three fingers. (*pointing at their legs*) Err . . . three, plus one . . .

CUDDY

Four!

DETRITUS

Four legs!

CUDDY

If you can count to two you can count to anything. And then – the world's your mollusc!

DETRITUS

The world's my mollusc! Er, what's a mollusc?

(The hooded man runs past them. He opens the trapdoor ('manhole') and drops out of sight)

CUDDY

Hi! You! Stop! In the name of the law! (*to Detritus*) He's gone into the sewers! Come on!

DETRITUS

Why we chase him?

CUDDY

Because he's running away!

(As they start to exit, the lights cross-fade to balcony. Colon is reading his report)

COLON

'At 10 a.m. today, I proceeded in the company of Corporal C.W.St John [*ie*, '*Sin-jun*'] Nobbs to the Guild of Fools and Joculators in God Street, whereupon we conversed with the clown Boffo who said the clown Beano, the corpus derelicti, was definitely seen by him, clown Boffo, leaving the Guild the previous morning just after the explosion.'

This is dead bent in my opinion, sir, the reason being the stiff was dead two days – me and Nobby agree on this– so someone is telling meat pies. Never trust anyone who falls on his bum for a living. Er, sir.

VIMES
Yes, carry on.

COLON
Also, clown Boffo went on about us looking for Beano's nose, but he had a nose on when we found him, so we said to clown Boffo did he mean a false nose and he said no, a real one.

VIMES
Why ask us to look for a nose that wasn't lost?

(*Colon shrugs*)

Look at this. (*he holds out the tubes*) It's part of some kind of new weapon. But why didn't the Assassins destroy it? No, that's not human nature, is it? Sometimes things are too fascinating to destroy. The Patrician must have known . . .

(*Captain Quirke enters*)

QUIRKE
Captain Vimes?

VIMES

Quirke? What are you doing here?

QUIRKE

You've got to come with me. And don't be a fool, Vimes.
You'd be a fool to resist arrest.

VIMES

What? I'm under arrest?

QUIRKE

You will be if you don't come with me and my men.
Come on, Vimes.

(They exit, leaving Colon, as the lights black out)

SCENE 12 – INSIDE THE PORK FUTURES WAREHOUSE

The stage is lit by a cold blue light. If you can manage it, some dry ice, or perhaps a little stage smoke, might be effective, too. Detritus is on stage by the open trap. Cuddy is just emerging.

CUDDY
Where are we?

DETRITUS
Pork futures warehouse.

(*Klaxon. Footnote enters*)

FOOTNOTE
Probably no other world in the multiverse has warehouses for things which only exist 'in potentia', but the pork futures warehouse in Ankh-Morpork's Shades . . .

(*A couple of 'parps' from an old-fashioned horn. The Footnote freezes. Another Footnote – a rather vicious old man of the Albert Steptoe persuasion – totters on, muttering to himself*)

FOOTNOTE #2 (*as he enters*)
Hah! Oh, yes . . . I'd have bin number one Footnote 'cept I din't go round waggling my bottom, unlike some as I could mention . . . (*he casts a baleful glare at the Footnote, who while remaining frozen, is contriving to look none too*

pleased at this interruption!) Now then, what did I come out here for? Oh yes, the Shades. (*clears throat*) Every city in the multiverse has its more, er, picturesque quarter and Ankh-Morpork's is called the Shades. It is the abode of discredited gods and unlicensed thieves; ladies of the night and pedlars in exotic goods. In short, the grease on civilisation's axle and the unidentifiable sticky stuff on the sole of its boots. Back to you, Miss Clever.

(*With a disdainful sneer at the Footnote, he 'parps' again and exits. The Footnote unfreezes*)

FOOTNOTE

As I was saying . . . Probably no other world in the multiverse has warehouses for things which only exist 'in potentia', but the pork futures warehouse in Ankh-Morpork's Shades is a product of the Patrician's rules about baseless metaphors, the literal-mindedness of citizens who assume that everything must exist somewhere, and the general thinness of the fabric of reality around Ankh, which is so thin that it's as thin as a very thin thing. The net result is that trading in pork futures – in pork that doesn't exist yet – led to the building of a warehouse to store it until it does.

(*Klaxon. Footnote exits*)

DETRITUS (*thicko voice*)

Come on then. Oh dear. Used to work here. Used to work everywhere. 'Go away, you stupid troll, you too thick'.

CUDDY
    Is there another way out?

DETRITUS (*more intelligent voice*)
    No. The street door is heavily bolted and padlocked
    from the outside. No-one comes in here for months at a
    time.

CUDDY (*shivering*)
    You in there! It's the Watch! Step out now!

    (*A shot is fired. Cuddy falls. Three more shots! Each hits
    Detritus, who also falls over. Then the robed figure enters
    and ducks down the trap, pulling it shut behind him.
    Detritus crosses to the trap and tries to open it. It has been
    bolted from the other side. He crosses to Cuddy*)

DETRITUS
    You alive?

CUDDY (*sitting up*)
    Yeah. It just grazed me.

DETRITUS (*chairman of MENSA voice*)
    It looks like a mild skin abrasion.

CUDDY
    You what? What about you?

DETRITUS
    I suppose the armour was some help. If it hadn't slowed
    the projectiles down somewhat then I might have been
    seriously abraded.

CUDDY

What's up with you? Why are you talking like that? The manhole!

DETRITUS

It's bolted. And the doors are troll-proof. So we're stuck. I say, I do believe that I am genuinely cogitating. Of course! Superconductivity!

CUDDY

I think I'm going to freeze to death soon. Wha' you on about?

DETRITUS

Troll, you see? Brain of impure silicon. Problem of heat dissipation. Daytime temperature too hot, processing speed slows down, weather gets hotter, brain stops completely, trolls go still as a stone till nightfall. However, lower temperature . . . brain works faster – so in cold store, can think as fast as you warm-blooded types. (*he looks into a side room*) Oh dear.

CUDDY

What is it?

DETRITUS (*pulling out a body*)

This is genuinely quite a poser. I think we've found another body. Another dead clown.

CUDDY

What? (*he looks*) He looks just like the one we found before. It's Brother Beano. Again!

DETRITUS

Yes. This is very strange: the Fools' Guild have already buried him. Captain Vimes will need to know. And – we have to get you out of here, since the cold isn't as beneficial to you. There's a skylight up there. I reckon I can throw you through it – you'll land outside and you can get someone to force the door and release me.

Right (*he grabs Cuddy*) So, here we go!

(*Lights black out*)

CUDDY (*In the dark*)

Noo-oo-oo!!!

(*tinkle of glass*)

(*scene ends*)

SCENE 13 – THE OBLONG OFFICE

The Patrician is on stage, staring out at the audience. Vimes enters and salutes. The Patrician does not acknowledge this.

PATRICIAN
Ah, Vimes. Come here, will you? And tell me what you see.

VIMES (*coming down to him*)
City of Ankh-Morpork, sir.

PATRICIAN
And does it put you in mind of anything, Captain?

VIMES
Well, sir, when I was a kid we owned a cow once, and one day it got sick, and it was always my job to clean out the cowshed, and . . .

PATRICIAN
It reminds me of a clock. Big wheels, little wheels. All clicking away. The little wheels spin and the big wheels turn, all at different speeds, you see, but the machine works. And that is the most important thing. The machine keeps going. Because when the machine breaks down . . .

(*he moves away from the 'window'*)

Or, again, sometimes a bit of grit might get into the wheels, throwing them off balance. One speck of grit. (*he turns to Vimes and smiles, mirthlessly*) I won't have that. (*pause*) I believe I told you to forget about certain recent events, Captain?

VIMES
Sir.

PATRICIAN
Yet it appears that the Watch have been getting in the wheels.

VIMES
Sir.

PATRICIAN
What am I to do with you?

VIMES
Couldn't say, sir.

PATRICIAN
Captain Vimes, you have no concept of the delicate balance of the city. I'll tell you one more time. This business with the Assassins and the dwarf and this clown . . . you are to cease involving yourself.

VIMES
No sir, I can't.

PATRICIAN
Give me your badge.

VIMES
My . . . badge?

PATRICIAN
And your sword.

(*Vimes hands him the sword*)

And your badge.

VIMES
Um. Not my badge.

PATRICIAN
Why not?

VIMES
Um. Because it's my badge.

PATRICIAN
But you're resigning anyway when you get married.

VIMES
Right. (*he meets the Patrician's eyes*)

PATRICIAN
It means that much to you? (*pause*) Very well. Yes. You
can keep your badge. And have an honourable re-
tirement. The Day Watch will be sent down to the Yard
shortly to disarm your men. I'm standing down the
Night Watch, Captain. I may appoint another man in
charge in due course. Until then your men can consider
themselves on leave.

VIMES
The Day Watch? A bunch of . . .

PATRICIAN
I'm sorry?

VIMES
Yes, sir.

PATRICIAN
One infraction, however, and the badge is mine. Remember.

> (*Vimes exits. He does not bang the door jamb. The Patrician moves to another door and speaks, off*)

Leonard. Would you come in now?

> (*Leonard of Quirm enters. Although we had most citizens dressed in Georgian clothes, Leonard, of course, was dressed in the Italian Renaissance style*)

LEONARD OF QUIRM
My Lord?

> (*Klaxon. Footnote enters*)

FOOTNOTE
Leonard of Quirm is probably the most dangerous man on the Discworld. He is an artist and an inventor. His true genius lies in seeing inherent in the common world the obvious things that men have never seen before. He watches the swirl of water over weirs, the intricate

movements of musculature, the gliding of birds and then, fills up notebook after notebook with ingenious devices for killing whole cities by means of hot oil, explosions, etc. He has never in his life harmed a living creature, and would be greatly surprised and terribly shocked to think that anyone would take these doodles, with their carefully numbered components and cutaway diagrams, seriously. Inventions of his, lying unnoticed in obscure places or as idle sketches in the margins of otherwise unremarkable books, lie around Ankh-Morpork like razor blades in the ham sandwich of time.

(*Klaxon. Footnote exits*)

PATRICIAN
What have you got there?

LEONARD OF QUIRM
These are my cartoons, my Lord.

PATRICIAN (*browsing through them*)
Very good. I like this one of the boy going sledging with a toy tiger. There's a piece of yellow paper stuck to this one.

(*He takes it off. It sticks to his finger*)

LEONARD OF QUIRM
Oh, I'm rather pleased with that one. I call it my Handy-note-scribbling-piece-of-paper-with-glue-that-comes-unstuck-when-you-want.

PATRICIAN

For a man who is such a genius at inventing things, I never cease to be amazed at your total inability to come up with catchy names for things. What's the glue made of?

LEONARD OF QUIRM

Boiled slugs. What was it you wanted to see me about?

PATRICIAN

I wanted to talk to you about . . . the gonne. The thing you called The-you-point-it-and-the-enemy-is-gonne-stick.

LEONARD OF QUIRM

Oh dear.

PATRICIAN

I am afraid it has . . . escaped.

LEONARD OF QUIRM

My goodness. I thought you said you'd done away with it.

PATRICIAN

I gave it to the Assassins to destroy. After all, they take pride in the artistic quality of their work. They should be horrified at the idea of just anyone having that sort of power. But they did not destroy it. They thought they could lock it away. And now they've lost it.

LEONARD OF QUIRM
They didn't destroy it?

PATRICIAN
Apparently not, the damned fools.

LEONARD OF QUIRM
And nor did you. I wonder why?

PATRICIAN
I . . . I do not know.

LEONARD OF QUIRM
I should never have made it. It was merely an application of principles. Ballistics, you know. Simple aerodynamics. Chemical power. Some rather good alloying, although I say it myself. And I'm rather proud of the rifling idea. I had to make quite a complicated tool for that. (*pause*) People are searching for it, I trust?

PATRICIAN
The Assassins are. But they won't find it. They don't think the right way. (*pause*) So I am relying on the Watch.

LEONARD OF QUIRM
This would be the Captain Vimes you have spoken of. I hope you have impressed upon him the importance of the task.

PATRICIAN

In a way. I've absolutely forbidden him to undertake it. Twice.

LEONARD OF QUIRM

Ah. I . . . think I understand. I hope it works. (*he sighs*) I suppose I should have dismantled it. I remember I had this strange fancy that I was merely assembling something that already existed. It seemed . . . somehow . . . sacrilege, I suppose, to dismantle it. It'd be like dismantling a person.

PATRICIAN

Dismantling a person is sometimes necessary.

LEONARD OF QUIRM

This is, of course, a point of view.

PATRICIAN

There is in this city a man with a gonne. He has used it successfully once and almost succeeded a second time. (*pause*) This city, you know, runs like clockwork. Occasionally you hope that if you wind the spring one way, all its energies will unwind the other way. And sometimes you have to wind the spring as tight as it will go. And pray it doesn't break. (*pause*) Oh dear.

LEONARD OF QUIRM

Mmm?

PATRICIAN

He was too depressed to thump the door arch. I may have gone too far.

(Lights black out)

INTERVAL

SCENE 14 – THE WATCH HOUSE

Detritus is on stage, shivering. Cuddy is holding a blanket around him and offering him a mug of hot lava. Carrot is showing Angua a reference in the Laws & Ordinances.

CUDDY
How many fingers am I holding up?

DETRITUS
Two and one?

CUDDY
It'll do for a start.

DETRITUS
One clown . . . two bodies. Now that doesn't add up!

(Colon enters, supporting Vimes, who is not wearing his armour. Vimes holds a whisky bottle)

CARROT
Captain! What's the matter with him? Has he been drinking?

COLON
Only a couple of whiskies. Trouble is, I don't think he's been drinking on an empty stomach. I think he put some alcohol in it first.

CARROT

He promised he wouldn't drink any more! He must have had a whole bottle.

ANGUA

It's CMOT Dibbler's Soggy Mountain Dew. He's going to die! It says one hundred and fifty per cent proof!

COLON

Nah, that's just old Dibbler's advertising. It ain't got no proof. Just circumstantial evidence! Ere, 'old on. Why hasn't he got his sword?

VIMES

Aargh! Swor? Gi' it away! Hooray!

COLON

What?

VIMES

No mo' Watsh! All go—

CARROT

I think he's a bit drunk.

VIMES

Drun'? 'm not drun'! You wouldn' dare call m'drun' if I was sober.

COLON

Blimey. I haven't seen him like this for years. Here, let me try something. Want another drink, Captain?

ANGUA
He certainly doesn't need another—

COLON
Shut up, I know what I'm doing. Want another drink, Captain?

VIMES
Mm?

COLON
I've never known him not be able to give a clear 'yes'. I think we'd better get him up to his bed.

CARROT
I'll take him.

(*Lights cross-fade to Vimes' room. Carrot takes Vimes over and lays him on the bed*)

COLON (*to Detritus & Cuddy*)
You two! Go next door and get some Klatchian Coffee. That'll bring him back up to sobriety.

VIMES
All go 'way! Bang! bang!

COLON
Lady Ramkin's not going to be happy.

ANGUA
Is this it? Is this where he lives? It's so bare!

COLON
   Yes, miss, er, Lance-Constable. What did you expect?

ANGUA
   I don't know. A picture? A rug? Anything? (*To Carrot*)
   How can you admire a man like this?

CARROT
   He's a very fine man.

   (*Angua starts to look in a cardboard box by Vimes' bed*)

   Hey, I don't think you should do that.

ANGUA
   I'm just looking. No law against that.

CARROT
   In fact, under the Privacy Act of 1467, it is an—

ANGUA
   There's not much, anyway.

   (*She takes out a battered notebook*)

   Will you look at this? No wonder he never has any
   money!

CARROT
   What do you mean?

ANGUA
   He spends it on women! You wouldn't think it, would
   you? Look at this entry. Four in one week!

Mrs Gaskin, Mincing Street, five dollars.

Mrs Skurrick, Treacle Street, four dollars.

Mrs Maroon, Wixon's Allay, four dollars.

Annabel Curry, Lobsneaks, two dollars.

Annabel Curry couldn't have been much good, for only two dollars.

CARROT

> (*The temperature in the room has dropped quite markedly*)

I shouldn't think so. She's only nine years old.

> (*He grabs her wrist and prises out the book*)

Sergeant! Could you come over here a moment?

> (*Colon crosses to them. Cuddy and Detritus follow part of the way*)

Sergeant, Lance-Constable Angua wants to know about Mrs Gaskin.

COLON
Old Leggy Gaskin's widow? She lives in Mincing Street. Takes in laundry now.

CARROT
How about Annabel Curry?

COLON (*still not clear what's going on*)
She still goes to the Spiteful Sisters of Seven-Handed
Sek Charity School, doesn't she? She's the daughter of
old Corporal Curry. He was before your time. But
why . . . ?

ANGUA
They're the widows of coppers?

CARROT
And one orphan.

COLON
It's a tough old life. No pensions for widows, see. Sam
worries a lot about that. Is there something wrong?

CARROT
No.

(*He puts the book back in the box*)

ANGUA
Look, I'm sorry . . . But, fourteen dollars . . . that's nearly
half his pay! I mean . . . half his pay!

CARROT
Forget it.

(*Cuddy & Detritus enter, with the coffee. Colon takes it
and gives it to Vimes. They all put their fingers in their
ears. Vimes drinks it and instantly comes out of drunken-
ness, through sobriety and out the other side*)

VIMES
Aaargh!

(*They all take their fingers out of their ears*)

Where am I? Oh. Right. Now – we're off the case.

ALL
What?

VIMES
The Patrician's given the whole bloody lot to Captain
Quirke. He's already arrested Coalface the troll.

COLON
What? Old 'Mayonnaise' Quirke?

ANGUA
'Mayonnaise'? Don't tell me . . . it's because he's thick
and oily, right?

CARROT
And smells faintly of eggs.

COLON
But why's he arrested Coalface? He's a villain, all right,
but he's not a killer.

VIMES
Who knows? Who cares?

CUDDY

But Captain, we've found another body. A clown. In the old pork futures warehouse.

VIMES

And?

CUDDY

It's not just any old clown! It's BROTHER BEANO! He's dead again!

VIMES

So what? It's Captain Quirke's problem, now. Listen to me. Supposing we'd found who killed the dwarf and the clown. Both of him. It wouldn't make any difference. It's all rotten. You might as well try to empty a well with a sieve. There's no place in Ankh-Morpork for policemen. Who cares what's right or wrong? Assassins and thieves and trolls and dwarfs! Might as well have a bloody king and be done with it!

CARROT

It's better to light a candle than to curse the darkness, Captain. That's what they say.

VIMES

WHAT? Who says so? When has that ever been true? It's never been true! It's the kind of thing that people without power say to make it all seem less bloody awful. But it's just words, it never makes any difference!

(*There is a knocking at the door*)

104

That'll be Quirke. He's running the show for the next 24 hours. Go and let him in, Lance-Constable Cuddy.

(*Cuddy does so. Quirke enters*)

QUIRKE

Well, well, well. Here we are. Nice place you lot have got here. What a pity you won't have the use of it. (*to Cuddy & Detritus*) Surprised to see you two here . . . I thought you'd be fighting up Quarry Lane with the rest of the rocks and gritsuckers. (*sarcastically*) Oops, sorry, forgot my manners there.

CARROT

Fighting? Why?

VIMES

Maybe it's got something to do with a wrongful arrest. Maybe it's got something to do with some of the more restless dwarfs just needing an excuse to have a go at the trolls. Maybe there's always some idiot ready to light matches in a firework factory. What do you think, Quirke?

QUIRKE

I don't think, Vimes.

VIMES

Good man. You're just the type the city wants.

(*He stands*)

I'll see you all tomorrow, then. If there is one.

105

(He exits)

QUIRKE

My gods, there'll be some changes here once I've taken over.

CARROT

What do you mean? The Patrician hasn't announced Captain Vimes' successor yet!

QUIRKE

Well, it's hardly likely to be one of you, is it? Seems to me it's likely the Watches'll be combined. Seems to me there's too much sloppiness around here. Seems to me that just about anything has been allowed to join the Night Watch. First thing that's needed'll be a good clearout. Now then, let's see what weapons you lot have got, eh?

(He exits into a side room)

CARROT

What's all this about fighting? (*he starts to look through his Law book*)

NOBBS

It's true. I saw it when I was on my way here. They say the trolls are planning to march to the Palace to get Coalface out. There's gangs of dwarfs and trolls wandering around the place looking for trouble.

Hey – and people threw stuff at me!

CARROT

Tell me, has there been an irretrievable breakdown of law and order?

COLON

Yeah, for about five hundred years. That's what Ankh-Morpork is all about.

CARROT

No. I mean more than usual. It's important.

NOBBS

Throwing stuff at me sounds like a breakdown in law and order.

COLON

I don't think we could make that stick.

NOBBS

It stuck all right. And some of it went down my shirt.

ANGUA

Why throw things at you?

NOBBS

Because I'm a Watchman.

COLON

That's not on, is it? Someone shoots something at Cuddy and Detritus, and he locks them in a cold store to try and kill 'em. Local citizens pelt Nobby with rotten fruit . . .

NOBBS
It wasn't just fruit, neither—

COLON
We've been stood down as the City's Night Watch, though, haven't we?

ANGUA
Yes, so . . .

COLON
That means we're not getting paid to be the whipping boys. That's Quirke's job. Come on lads, and Angua, school's out. To the pub!

(*With general murmurs of agreement, the Night Watch all exit*)

CARROT (*as he exits*)
But what I need to be sure is, does rotten fruit count as 'irretrievable breakdown'. It's important.

(*Quirke re-enters from the side room*)

QUIRKE
Right then, I'll be padlocking your weapons room, and . . . Sod me, they've buggered off!

(*Lights out*)

SCENE 15 – A BATHROOM IN LADY RAMKIN'S HOUSE

Set on a raised area. Steam. Noise of splashing. Vimes appears, in 'the bath'.

VIMES (*singing*)
Oooh! A wizard's staff has a nob on the end, a nob on the end, a nob on the end! A wizard's staff has a nob on the end, a nob on the end, a nob on the end!

City Watch? Who bloody cares, eh? Tomorrow I'll be Mr Ramkin. This'll be my bath. I'll have my own butler! Willikins! (*Willikins enters, carrying a back brush*) What's that for?

WILLIKINS
His lordship . . . that is, her Ladyship's father . . . he required to have his back scrubbed, sir.

VIMES
Not me, Willikins. I've always bathed myself. Both times. Ha, ha ha! (*no reaction*) That was a joke, Willikins.

WILLIKINS
Very droll, sir. I shall recount that one to Mrs Willikins this evening. It will help to pass the evening.

VIMES
Willikins, just how do the Ramkins manage to have piped hot water in their house, eh? Tell me that.

WILLIKINS
There were a number of hot springs in this area of the city, sir. This house has an ancient geyser in the cellar.

VIMES
What, and you help this old geyser to stoke the furnaces, eh? Ha!

WILLIKINS (*completely po-faced*)
Please, Captain Vimes, sir. I shall split my sides in a moment. Would sir be wanting anything?

VIMES
Well, a large glass of—

WILLIKINS
Lady Ramkin said you wouldn't be wanting any alcohol.

VIMES
Did she?

WILLIKINS
Emphatically, sir.

VIMES
In that case, Willikins, no, I want nothing. Willikins?

WILLIKINS
Sir?

VIMES

What's your first name?

WILLIKINS

First name, sir?

VIMES

I mean, what do people call you when they've got to know you better?

WILLIKINS

Willikins, sir.

VIMES

Oh. Right, then. Well. You may go, Willikins.

WILLIKINS (*exiting*)

Yes, sir. Thank you, sir.

VIMES (*sighing*)

Just about now I'd have been patrolling along the Street of Small Gods, or . . . stop it, Vimes. Forget it. Who bloody cares? (*sighing*) 'Oooh, a wizard when young has a staff that is small, Puny and thin, ineffective withal . . .'

(*As he sings, the lights black out*)

SCENE 16 – THE BUCKET, GLEAM STREET

*On stage are Angua, Carrot, Colon, Nobby, Cuddy &
Detritus. We hear the city's clocks chiming again.*

NOBBS

What say we have a game of cards?

COLON

You won everyone's wages off them yesterday. You had
five kings.

NOBBS

S'funny that. There's kings everywhere, when you look.

ANGUA

There certainly is if you look up your sleeve!

NOBBS

No, I mean, there's King's Way in Ankh, and kings in
cards, and we get the King's Shilling when we join up
. . . we got kings all over the place except on the golden
throne in the Palace. I tell you . . . there wouldn't be all
this trouble if we had a king.

COLON

Oh yeah . . . beer'd be a penny a pint, the trees'd bloom
again. Vimes'd go spare to hear you talk like that.

DETRITUS

How'd you getta king inna first place?

COLON

Someone sawed up a stone.

DETRITUS

Hah! Anti-siliconism!

ANGUA

No, someone pulled a sword *out* of a stone. Only the rightful king could do it, see?

COLON

Hah! Anyone could take a sword out a stone. You'd need more than a man who can pull swords out of stones to rule this city. Seems to me a proper king'd been the one who could push it right in there in the first place!

NOBBS

Yeah. Man like that wouldn't be just a king, he'd be an ace.

(*We hear Vimes' watch chiming. Think of that watch chime from 'The Good, the Bad and the Ugly'*)

What's that?

(*Carrot pulls out the watch in its box*)

It's a clock?

CARROT
A watch.

ANGUA
And it plays a tune!

CARROT
Every hour. It's part of the mechanism.

ANGUA
It's slow, then. All the others just struck.

NOBBS
Oh, time's a bit of a wossname, consensus here, Miss. You must have heard. Every Guild's got its own clock tower and its own idea of what's the right time. Know what I think? The Watch is the only one that knows what time it really is. Gettit? The Watch, see? The watch! Oh, all right, please yourselves.

ANGUA
What's this inscription? 'To Captain Vimes. A Watch From, (*comma in the wrong place*) Your Old Freinds (*E and I the wrong way round*) in the Watch?'

CARROT
It's a play on words. (*embarrassed silence*) Um. I chipped in a few dollars each from you new recruits. I mean . . . you can pay me back when you like. If you want to. I mean . . . you'd be bound to be friends. Once you'd got to know him.

I was hoping we could give it to him tonight. And all go out for . . . a drink.

ANGUA
Not a good idea.

COLON
Leave it till tomorrow. We'll form a guard of honour at the wedding.

ANGUA
It's not fair. I don't care who stole whatever they stole from the Assassins, but he was right to try and find out who killed Mr Hammerhock. And Beano.

NOBBY
Twice. Beats me why anyone would be daft enough to steal from the Assassins. Captain Vimes said you'd have to be a fool to think of breaking into that place.

DETRITUS
What? Like a clown or a jester, you mean?

CARROT
Detritus, he didn't mean a cap-and-bells Fool. He just meant that you'd have to be some sort of idi—

Oh my. It's as simple as that?

ANGUA
Simple as what?

QUIRKE (*offstage*)
Help! Help!

(*He bursts on*)

Good, I thought you lot'd be here! You must help!
They've attacked the Watch House!

CARROT
Who has?

QUIRKE (*indicating Detritus*)
Them! The trolls!

CARROT
This isn't a troll. This is Lance-Constable Detritus –
don't salute! – You're saying Trolls attacked the Watch
House?

(*He pulls out his copy of the Laws*)

QUIRKE
They're chucking cobbles! There's gangs of trolls and
dwarfs running riot in the city. Our women won't be
safe! You know what they say about dwarfs!

DETRITUS
You can't trust 'em.

CARROT
Who?

DETRITUS
Trolls. Nasty pieces of work in my opinion. They need
keeping an eye on.

CUDDY
What do they say about dwarfs?

QUIRKE
You've got to do something!

CUDDY
Detritus, what do they say about dwarfs?

COLON
We're stood down. Official.

CUDDY
Sergeant Colon, what do—

QUIRKE
Don't give me that!

CUDDY
Corporal Carrot, what do—

CARROT
Ah. Erm, do you still have that little house in Easy
Street, Captain Quirke?

QUIRKE
What? What? Yes! What about it?

CARROT
Is the rent more than a farthing a month?

QUIRKE
Are you simple, or what?

CARROT
That's right, Captain. Is it though? Worth a farthing, would you say?

QUIRKE
There's dwarfs and trolls running havoc all over the city and you want to know about property prices?

CARROT
A farthing?

QUIRKE
Don't be daft! It's worth at least five dollars a month!

CARROT
Ah. And I expect you've got a cooking pot . . . do you own at least two-and-one-thirds acres of land and more than half a cow?

QUIRKE
All right, all right. It's some kind of joke, yes?

CUDDY
Captain Quirke, what is it they say about dwarfs?

CARROT
I think the property qualifications can be waived. It says that it can be waived for a citizen of good standing. Finally, has there been, in your opinion, an irreparable breakdown of law and order?

QUIRKE
They turned over Dibbler's barrow and made him eat two of his sausages-in-a-bun!

COLON
Oh, I say!

QUIRKE
Without mustard!

CARROT
I think we can call that a yes. (*closing his book with a snap*) I think we'd better be going.

ANGUA
But we've been stood down.

CARROT
According to the Laws and Ordinances of Ankh-Morpork, any resident of the city, in times of irreparable breakdown of law and order, shall, at the request of an officer of the city who is a citizen of good standing – there's a lot of stuff about property and such – form themselves into a militia for city defence.

ANGUA
  What does that mean?

COLON
  Militia?

QUIRKE
  Hang on! You can't do that. That's nonsense!

CARROT
  It's the law. We've got to stop the riot. And we can start
  by finding the real murderer. We're going into the
  Fools' Guild.

COLON
  Why there?

CARROT
  It backs onto the Assassins' Guild. They're going to give
  me some answers. They haven't told me the truth.

COLON
  I don't see . . . OK, OK. But no violence, Carrot. I'm still
  the Sergeant around here. If Doctor Whiteface won't
  speak to you, you're to leave peacefully, OK?

CARROT
  If he won't answer my questions, I'm to leave peacefully.
  Right.

COLON (*as they all exit*)
  That's a direct order, Corporal!

CUDDY
  Sergeant Colon. What is it . . . ?

  (*As they exit, Colon whispers to Cuddy. Cuddy looks shocked. Colon exits. Cuddy — alone on stage, peers into the top of his breeches, and then exits. Lights black out, and come up again almost immediately on . . .*)

SCENE 17 – THE FOOLS' GUILD

We hear a doorbell clanging away. Brother Boffo crosses the stage hurriedly and goes to answer it. As he opens the door a hand comes out and smacks him in the face with a custard pie. Immediately, Carrot enters, followed by Colon, Angua, Nobby, Cuddy & Detritus; each, as they enter, push a custard pie into Boffo's face.

BOFFO
Ow! What was that for?

CARROT
Good day, to you. We just wanted to get into the spirit of the thing. I'm Corporal Carrot of the City's militia, and we all enjoy a good laugh.

CUDDY
'Scuse me . . .

CARROT
Except for Lance-Constable Cuddy. We're here to see Dr Whiteface.

BOFFO
Have . . . have you an appointment?

CARROT
I don't know. Have we got an appointment?

NOBBS
I got an iron ball with spikes on.

CARROT
That's a morningstar, Nobby. An appointment is an engagement to see someone, while a morningstar is just a large lump of metal used for crushing skulls. It is important not to confuse the two, isn't it Mr . . . ?

BOFFO
Boffo, sir. But—

(*Dr Whiteface bursts on*)

DR WHITEFACE
There is no such thing as a city militia, Corporal. What's going on? Well?

CARROT
Good day, Doctor.

DR WHITEFACE
I should like to make it clear that Lord Vetinari will be hearing about this directly.

CARROT
Oh yes. I shall tell him.

DR WHITEFACE
I can't imagine why you're bothering me when there's rioting in the streets.

CARROT

Ah well . . . we shall deal with that later. But Captain Vimes always told me, sir, that there are big crimes and little crimes. Sometimes the little crimes look big and the big crimes you can hardly see, but the crucial thing is to decide which is which.

DR WHITEFACE

Well?

CARROT

I should like you to tell me about events in this Guild House the night before last.

DR WHITEFACE

And if I choose not to?

CARROT

Then I am afraid I shall, with extreme reluctance, be forced to carry out the order I was given just before we got here. That's right, isn't it, sergeant?

COLON

What? Eh? Well, yes—

CARROT

I would much prefer not to, but I would have no choice.

DR WHITEFACE

But this is Guild property! You have no right to—

CARROT

I don't know about that, I'm only a Corporal. But I've never disobeyed a direct order yet, and I am sorry to say that I will carry this one out fully and to the letter.

DR WHITEFACE

Now see here—

CARROT

If it's any comfort, I'll probably be ashamed about it.

DR WHITEFACE

Listen! If I shout, I can have a dozen men in here!

CARROT

Believe me, that will only make it easier for me to obey.

DR WHITEFACE (*conceding defeat*)

Confound it! How did you find out, eh? Who told you?

CARROT

I really couldn't say. But it makes sense. There's only one entrance to each Guild and the Guild houses are back to back. Someone just had to have cut through the wall.

DR WHITEFACE

I assure you we didn't know about it. We thought it was just a prank. We thought young Beano had done it with humorous intent, and then he turned up dead and . . .

CARROT

You'd better show me the hole.

DR WHITEFACE

It's in Beano's old room. Through here.

(*He exits. As Carrot goes to follow him, Colon grabs his arm*)

COLON

I've seen people bluff on a bad hand, boy, but I've never seen anyone bluff with no cards!

(*Carrot disappears into the room. After a moment, he re-enters, with Whiteface*)

CARROT

It's just a student assassin's bedroom on the other side, sergeant. No-one's been in there for a while, though. There's dust all over the floor, but there's footprints in it. (*to Whiteface*) Now, let me just understand this. Beano – or perhaps someone looking like Beano – made a hole into the Assassins' Guild, yes? And then went through and exploded that dragon? And then he came back through that hole? So how did he get killed?

DR WHITEFACE

By the Assassins, surely. They'd be within their rights. Trespass on Guild property is a very serious offence.

CARROT

Did anyone see Beano after the explosion?

DR WHITEFACE
Brother Boffo did.

CARROT
He knew it was him?

DR WHITEFACE
Of course he did! He recognised him, of course. That's how you know who people are. It's called re-cog-ni-tion. He said that he looked very worried.

CARROT
Fine, did Beano have any friends among the assassins?

DR WHITEFACE
Possibly. We don't discourage visitors. Well, if there's nothing more . . .

CARROT
You don't want to lay a complaint against the Assassins for killing one of your members, then?

DR WHITEFACE (*with a hint of panic*)
What? No, no, certainly not. I mean, if an assassin broke into our Guild, I mean, not on proper business, well, we'd definitely consider we were well within our rights to . . .

ANGUA
Pour jelly into his shirt?

COLON
Hit him on the head with a bladder on a stick?

DR WHITEFACE
Possibly, yes. Well, if you don't need me . . .

CARROT
There was one more thing, Doctor. Might I have a look at Brother Beano's egg?

DR WHITEFACE
Egg?

CARROT
Yes. I've done a lot of reading about the City's institutions. Isn't it the case that every clown has to register their face with the Guild?

DR WHITEFACE
Er, yes, erm, Brother Boffo!

BOFFO (*entering*)
Yes, Doctor Whiteface?

DR WHITEFACE
Will you fetch Brother Beano's face for the Corporal.

BOFFO
Yes, doctor.

DR WHITEFACE
Oh, and Brother . . . ?

BOFFO
Yes, doctor?

(*Dr Whiteface squirts him in the face with a trick flower*)

Thank you, doctor.

(*He ducks out*)

DR WHITEFACE
Goodbye, Corporal. Sergeant. Madam.

(*He goes*)

ANGUA
Lance-Constable!

COLON
We'll see you back at the Watch House then, Corporal.

ANGUA
I'll stay. I'd like to see what's going on.

(*Colon and co. leave, leaving just Angua and Carrot.
Boffo re-enters, with a painted egg*)

BOFFO
Here. This is Brother Boffo's face.

CARROT
Are you often on gate duty, Boffo?

BOFFO
Huh! All the time.

CARROT

So when did that friend of his, you know, the Assassin . . . visit him?

BOFFO

Oh. You know about him, then? About 10 days ago.

CARROT

He'd forgotten Beano's name, hadn't he, but he knew the room. Couldn't remember the number but he went straight to it.

BOFFO

Yes. I suppose Dr Whitehouse told you.

CARROT (*choosing his words carefully*)

I have spoken to Dr Whitehouse. So this is Brother Beano, eh? (*taking the egg*) Very valuable thing, a clown's face.

BOFFO

Yes.

ANGUA

What happens if a clown wants to use another clown's face?

BOFFO

Oh, we compare each new design with all the other eggs in the museum. It's not allowed.

CARROT
But supposing . . . that a clown, I mean a clown with his own face . . . supposing he used another clown's face?

BOFFO
Pardon?

ANGUA
Supposing you used another clown's make-up.

BOFFO
Oh, that happens all the time. People're always borrowing each other's slap . . .

ANGUA
Slap?

CARROT
Make-up. No, I think what the Lance-Constable is asking, Boffo, is: could a clown make himself up to look like another clown?

BOFFO
Sorry?

ANGUA
Couldn't you wake up one morning and put on make-up so that you looked like a different clown?

BOFFO (*horrified*)
But how could I do that? Then I wouldn't be me!

ANGUA
Someone else might do it, though.

BOFFO
I don't have to stay here and listen to this dirty talk, miss!

CARROT
Sorry. I think I understand. Now, when we found poor Mr Beano, he didn't have his clown wig on, but something like that could easily have fallen off into the river. But his nose, now. You told Sergeant Colon that someone had taken his nose. His real nose. Could you point to your real nose, Boffo?

(*Boffo taps his false nose*)

ANGUA
But that's—

CARROT
Your real nose, yes. Thank you Boffo.

(*He hands him back the egg*)

BOFFO
Right, well. If that's everything? Goodbye.

(*He exits*)

ANGUA
So what did happen, Carrot?

CARROT

This, I think. Someone in the Assassins' Guild wanted a way of getting out and in without being stopped, because they guard their Guild very carefully. He realised that only a thin wall separated his room from the Fools' Guild. He only had to find out who lived on the other side. Later on, he killed Beano and took his wig and nose. He walked into the Guild made up as Beano. He cut through the wall. Then he strolled down to the museum, dressed as an Assassin, and stole the gonne. He came through the wall again, dressed up as Beano, and strolled away. And then . . . someone killed him, too.

ANGUA

Boffo said Beano looked worried.

CARROT

Yes, but he thinks of the make-up as the real face. The killer must've put the make-up on hurriedly, and got part of it crooked.

ANGUA

What now, then?

CARROT

We have to find out whose room is the one on the other side of Beano's.

ANGUA

The Assassins' Guild? On our own?

(*She glances up at the darkening sky*)

What time is it?

CARROT

Perhaps you're right . . . um . . .

(*He takes out Vimes' watch. The tune plays*)

A quarter to seven. Moon'll be up soon.

ANGUA

Right, erm. Look! I think I can find out.

CARROT

You? How?

ANGUA

Er, well, I could get out of uniform, couldn't I and, oh, erm, talk my way in as a kitchen maid's sister or something . . . Can you think of anything better?

CARROT

Well . . . no.

ANGUA

Right. You go back to the rest of the men. I'll find somewhere to change into something more suitable.

CARROT

Where can you get a change of clothes round here?

ANGUA

A good Watchman is always prepared. Go on. I'll see you later.

CARROT
  If you're sure.

ANGUA
  Yes!

  (*Carrot exits. Angua looks anxiously up at the moon*)

Most of the Assassins come from high-class families. The place is full of big shaggy hunting dogs. Another one won't attract much attention.

Oh dear. I wish Carrot could understand. It's not easy, being a werewolf. When it's that time of the month, you can't stay in to wash your hair.

  (*'Blue Moon' starts. Angua rushes off-stage. Immediately there is a howl. The werewolf lopes across the stage and heads for the Assassins' Guild*)

  (*Lights out*)

SCENE 18 – THE TOP OF THE TOWER OF ART

Wind noise throughout. On stage is the hooded figure. He is tinkering with the gonne. His voice is husky.

HOODED FIGURE
Blast Vimes! Why on earth did he have to run towards the shots? I lost a spare magazine because of that. Still. Still got three left. A bag of No.1 powder and a rudimentary knowledge of lead casting is all a man needs to rule the city . . . But you killed Hammerhock! d'Eath said you fired yourself! But he'd repaired you!

VOICE OF THE GONNE
What did you expect? Gratitude? He would have made another gonne! He was making sketches.

HOODED FIGURE
Was that a reason to kill him?

VOICE OF THE GONNE
Certainly. You have no understanding. One gonne is power.

HOODED FIGURE
How can I hear you speak? d'Eath said he could hear you speak. In his head. I didn't want to kill him.

VOICE OF THE GONNE
   Don't be so pathetic! I am a gonne! I was created only to kill! That is why we are here. From the top of this Tower we will have an excellent view of our target.

HOODED MAN
   Captain Vimes. Yes. Vimes deserves to die.

VOICE OF THE GONNE
   Vimes? Vimes? You dolt. We have a more important target than some drink-sodden pathetic excuse for a policeman.

HOODED MAN
   But who . . . ?

VOICE OF THE GONNE
   The Patrician!

   (*Lights out*)

SCENE 19 – THE WATCH HOUSE

Carrot is sat on Vimes' bed, writing a letter. We hear his written words over the speakers.

CARROT'S VOICE
Dearest Mum and Dad, I hope you are well. I have been very busy looking for whoever has been killing people by making holes in them.

There was a riot at the Palace and I released Coalface the troll. I did not know what to do with the rioters so I enrolled them into the Watch, 'cos as Corporal Nobbs says it's better to have them inside pissing on each other than outside pissing on me. So now we have made Detritus a corporal in charge of training and we have lots of trolls and dwarfs and even undead people, vampires and suchlike, although not many because you know how I feel about people of their sort. I have met a new friend. Her name is Angua—

(Angua enters. She is dressed in a sheet)

ANGUA
Oh!

CARROT
Oh! What's happened to you?

ANGUA

I, er . . . my uniform got stolen. Er . . . while I was in the Assassins' Guild. Spying.

CARROT

Was that your disguise?

ANGUA

No. No. But, er, I'd taken my disguise off and . . . er . . . thrown it over the wall when I realised that my own stuff had gone. I saw a tramp running off. He was muttering.

CARROT

'Buggrit?' 'Millennium hand and shrimp?'

ANGUA

Yes!

CARROT

That's Foul Ole Ron the beggar. He's harmless. I'll go round and get your uniform later. What did you find out?

ANGUA

Edward d'Eath was the person who stole the gonne. I think he killed Beano. Cruces is really upset. He's shouting orders to everyone. He's got assassins looking all over the city. We know someone killed Edward . . .

CARROT

And someone shot at Detritus and Cuddy. So we're looking . . .

ANGUA
    . . . for a third man.

    [*Zither music – 'The Third Man' – what else?*]

CARROT
    And there's no clues! There's just some man out there
    somewhere with a gonne! Where do we start looking?

    (*He returns to his letter*)

ANGUA
    Are you writing it all down, like Captain Vimes did?

CARROT
    No. I'm writing to my mum and dad.

COLON (*entering*)
    Oh, er, sorry, sir. What do you want me to do next?

CARROT
    Send them out in squads, sergeant. At least one human,
    one dwarf and one troll in each.

COLON
    Yessir. What'll they be doing?

CARROT
    They'll be being visible.

COLON
    Right. Sir? One of the volunteers, sir? It's Mr Bleakey,
    sir. From Elm Street? He's a vampire, sir. A decent sort.

It's not true all that business about virgins' necks. He works down at the kosher butchers. Public service, really . . .

CARROT
Thank him very much and send him home.

COLON
But—

CARROT
No undead, Sergeant.

COLON
Er . . . right. I'll . . . er . . . leave you to *it*, then . . .

(*With a knowing wink, he exits*)

ANGUA
They call you sir. Have you noticed?

CARROT
I know. It's not right. People ought to think for themselves, like Captain Vimes says. We'll hold the city together for the rest of the night. People've seen sense.

ANGUA
No. They've seen *you*. It's like hypnotism. People just seem to be prepared to do whatever you say. Because they like you.

(*sighs*)

Carrot?

CARROT (*busy at his letter*)
Hmm?

ANGUA
You know . . . when Cuddy and Detritus and me joined
the Watch – well, you know why it was us three, don't
you?

CARROT
Of course. Minority group representation. One dwarf,
one troll, one woman.

ANGUA
Ah. It wasn't exactly like that. You see, there's a lot of
undead in the city and the Patrician insisted that . . . oh
. . . it wouldn't work. I must be going.

CARROT
I'd . . . er . . . I'd like you to stay . . .

ANGUA
I *knew* you were going to say that. Oh, well. I guess it was
inevitable. Don't say anything, and it might just be all
right.

(*Just as they are about to kiss, we hear the Klaxon. The
action freezes. Footnote enters*)

FOOTNOTE
Er, I think we'll just draw a veil over these proceedings
before we encounter any problems with the censor.
Terrible things are about to occur. No, I don't mean
Corporal Carrot losing his . . . discovering about the

pleasures of the . . . erm, well, finding out about the . . . anyway, I don't mean that.

A young man and his young lady. Well it's all perfectly natural. Normally. Except that it's now several hours later and Carrot has just opened the curtains . . .

. . . letting the moonlight in.

(*We hear the wolf howl*)

You go to sleep next to a girl and wake up next to a wolf and end up chasing it down the street while wearing nothing but a frown. A thing like that puts a strain on any relationship.

(*Klaxon. Footnote exits. Scene changes*)

SCENE 20 – THE SQUARE OUTSIDE UNSEEN UNIVERSITY

Bells are pealing for Vimes' wedding. He and Lady Ramkin are on stage.

VIMES
You sure this is OK? My seeing the bride before the ceremony?

LADY RAMKIN
Of course, Samuel. We don't need luck.

VIMES
Well that's all right then, 'cos that's something I'm always out of. Oh, apart from meeting you, of course.

LADY RAMKIN (*thumping him playfully*)
Sam Vimes! You big softy!

VIMES
Who's giving you away, by the way?

LADY RAMKIN
Havelock.

VIMES
The Patrician? Oh, perfect!

LADY RAMKIN
And who are you having as Best Man?

VIMES
Best Man? Oh my gods, I forgot all about a best man!

LADY RAMKIN
Well, go and find one. You've got half an hour.

(*She breezes off*)

VIMES
It's not as easy as that, is it? I can't think who to ask!

(*Colon enters. With Detritus*)

Fred! Fred my old colleague. I need a best man.

COLON
Right, sir, I'll just get Corporal Carrot, he's just checking the rooftops—

VIMES
Fred! I've known you for more than twenty years! Good grief! All you have to do is stand there. Fred, you're good at that!

(*Carrot trots in*)

CARROT
Ah. Sergeant Colon. Is the guard of honour all sorted out?

VIMES
Guard of honour? What guard—

COLON
Yes sir. But I can't find Corporal Nobbs, sir.

CARROT
Will it matter if Corporal Nobbs isn't present?

COLON
Well, it'll make the guard of honour that bit smarter, sir.

CARROT
I've sent him on a special mission. He shouldn't be long.

VIMES
What special miss—?

COLON
I can't find Lance-Constable Cuddy—

CARROT
He's checking the Tower of Art.

COLON
Or Lance-Constable Angua either, sir.

(*Carrot puts his arm around Colon's shoulders and takes him to one side*)

CARROT
Sergeant? Did you know she was a werewolf?

COLON
Um . . . Captain Vimes sort of hinted, sir . . .

CARROT
How did he hint?

COLON (*glancing at Vimes*)
He sort of said: 'Fred, she's a damned werewolf. I don't like it any more than you do, but Vetinari says we've got to take one of them as well, and a werewolf's better than a zombie or a vampire.'

That's what he hinted, sir.

CARROT
I see. (*coldly*) Well, let's just get through the day, shall we? Go and check the rest of the Guard, Sergeant.

(*Colon salutes and exits. Carrot turns to Vimes*)

Sorry I'm late, sir. We really wanted this to be a surprise.

VIMES
A surprise? What did you want to be a surprise?

(*He sees something atop the Tower of Art*)

Who did you say you'd sent up the Tower of Art?

CARROT (*also looking*)
Lance-Constable Cuddy, sir. But he won't be there yet.

VIMES
Is he wearing black, Corporal?

CARROT
No sir. Regulation uniform as alwa . . . Oh, dear . . .

VIMES
I think our man is up there now, looking at us!

CARROT
But why doesn't he shoot?

VIMES
Because . . . we're not the target. There's someone more important than us attending the wedding, isn't there—

(*The Patrician enters*)

PATRICIAN
Ah, Vimes. Corporal Carrot. What a splendid day. One couldn't wish for better wea . . .

CARROT (*putting himself between the Patrician and the Tower*)
Look out, my Lord!

PATRICIAN
What?

VIMES
We have reason to believe that you are to be the killer's next victim! He's up there, on the Tower of Art.

PATRICIAN
Shooting at me, Vimes? From the top of the Tower of Art? Don't be ridiculous, man! It's over eight hundred feet high!

(*He pushes Carrot aside*)

You couldn't hit a barn door at that dist . . . .

(*A shot. The Patrician is hit [in the upper left chest] and falls to the ground. A second shot hits Carrot [in the head], who falls. Black out. In the dark, four more shots are heard*)

SCENE 21 – AN ALLEYWAY IN
ANKH-MORPORK

Colon enters. He sidles over to an alley entrance.

COLON
  Angua?

  (*There is a throaty growl off-stage*)

Right, er. Knew I'd find you sooner or later.

  (*The growl again*)

Look – You can rip out a man's jugular, I know . . .
wherever that is.

  (*Growl off-stage. Colon puts his hand to his throat*)

Oh yes, I remember now. (*clears his throat*) I can see you
. . . don't want to talk right now. He hasn't sent me,
you know. I come off me own bat, like. He's a good lad,
Carrot, but . . . well . . . he's got a bit to learn, sort of
thing.

  (*No response*)

And you're a wolf and human at the same time, right?
Tricky, that. I can see that. Bit of a dichotomy, sort of
thing. Makes you kind of like a dog, see. 'Cos that's what

dogs are – half wolf and half human. Half wild animal and half . . . well, sort of companion.

You can't run away from him. Not really. He's your 'master', see?

He wants you to come back. The thing is, if he finds you, that's it. He's got the upper hand. He'll speak: you'll have to obey. But you goes back of your own free will, then it's your decision. (*pause*) I don't want to have to come in there and get you. (*pause*) I really don't. (*pause*) Angua?

ANGUA
He drew his sword!

COLON
What did you expect? One minute the lad's on top of the world. He's got a whole new interest in life, something probably even better than going for long walks around the city (if memory serves), and then he turns round and sees this bloody great wolf – begging your pardon, no offence meant. I mean, you could've hinted. 'It's that time of the month', sort of thing. You can't blame him for being surprised, really.

ANGUA
I can't go back, I—

(*She freezes, tensing up*)

COLON
What? What?

ANGUA
He's been hurt!

(*She rushes off, ie the werewolf rushes out and across the stage*)

COLON (*following her*)
Here! Wait for me!

(*Lights out*)

SCENE 22 – THE SQUARE OUTSIDE UNSEEN UNIVERSITY AGAIN

On stage are the Patrician, Vimes, Detritus and Carrot, as for the end of Scene Twenty. Carrot has blood on his forehead from a graze. The Patrician is holding his arm.

LADY RAMKIN
Sam! What's happened?

(She moves across and helps the Patrician up)

VIMES
Detritus! Don't just stand there! Get some of the others and get over to that tower and see what's happening.

(Detritus exits)

LADY RAMKIN
Hell's teeth! What's done this to his arm?

VIMES
That's the gonne for you! Sort him out, will you, Sybil. And Corporal Carrot, too.

PATRICIAN
There's no need, Vimes, I assure you. It's just a flesh wound and of . . .

(He collapses again)

COLON
We can handle it, sir. We've got men on the roofs, and . . .

VIMES
Shut up! Stay here! That's an order! I'm going . . .

(*Detritus walks in, carrying Cuddy's body. He is followed by Colon, and Angua — who immediately crosses to Carrot. Detritus lays Cuddy carefully on the ground*)

COLON
We ran into Detritus on the way back here. We found Cuddy in the Tower of Art. He was on the floor. He must have been pushed off the stairs right at the top. Someone else was in there, too. Must've shinned down a rope. Caught me a right bang on the head.

CARROT
Being pushed off a tower's not worth it for a shilling.

VIMES
What's that in Cuddy's hand? (*he takes it*) A strip of black cloth.

COLON
Assassins wear that.

LADY RAMKIN
So do lots of other people. Black's black.

VIMES
You're right. Taking any action on the basis of this would be premature. You know, it'd probably get me fired.

(He waves the black fabric at the Patrician)

Assassins everywhere. On guard. You gave them the bloody gonne because you thought they were the best to guard it. You never thought of giving it to the guards!

DETRITUS
Aren't we going to give chase, Corporal Carrot?

VIMES
Chase who? He hit old Fred on the head and did a runner. He could trot around the corner, chuck the gonne over a wall, and who'd know? We don't know who we're looking for!

CARROT
I do.

I wondered how we could find him. We can't find him. So we make him find us. Captain, I want the sergeant to go out there and tell people we've got the killer.

VIMES
What?

CARROT
His name is Edward d'Eath. Say we've got him in custody. Say he was caught and badly injured, but he's alive.

VIMES
But we haven't . . .

CARROT
I don't like telling lies, Captain. But our man will have to go back through the sewers to the warehouse to see if the body's gone. Anyway, it's not your problem, sir.

VIMES
Isn't it? Why not?

CARROT
You're retiring in less than an hour. Do it, Sergeant Colon.

VIMES
Carrot, I still run the Watch! I'm the one supposed to give the orders.

CARROT
Sorry, Captain.

VIMES
So long as that's perfectly understood. Sergeant Colon?

COLON
Sir?

VIMES
Put out the news that we've arrested Edward d'Eath.

COLON
Sir!

VIMES
    Detritus, take Lance-Constable Cuddy back to the
    Watch House.

DETRITUS
    Yes, Captain.

    (*He picks up the body and exits. Nobby enters*)

NOBBS
    Wha—? What's happened here?

VIMES
    Nobby!

NOBBS
    Sir! What's happened to Cuddy . . . ?

VIMES
    No questions, Nobby. Not now. Stay here and guard
    Lady Ramkin.

NOBBS
    Yessir!

VIMES
    Sybil.

LADY RAMKIN
    Yes Samuel?

VIMES
Take care of his lordship, would you?

(*He gives her the black cloth*)

Use this. And take care of yourself. Corporal Carrot?
Back to the sewers and wait, eh?

(*They exit. A pause. Lady Ramkin puts a sling on the
Patrician's arm*)

NOBBS (*to the Patrician*)
What happened, my lord?

PATRICIAN
Who are you?

NOBBS
Corporal Nobbs, sir!

PATRICIAN
Do we employ you?

NOBBS
Yessir!

PATRICIAN
Ah. You're the dwarf, are you?

NOBBS
Nossir. That was the late Cuddy, sir! I'm one of the
human beings, sir!

PATRICIAN
You're not employed as the result of any . . . special hiring procedures?

NOBBS
Nossir!

PATRICIAN
My word.

(*Lights out*)

SCENE 23 – THE SEWERS

Water effect, stage swamped in green light, FX – dripping water. Carrot and Vimes, in heavy cloaks, are concealed on stage. Both have pistol crossbows. Vimes has a lantern. A black hooded figure enters and starts to cross the stage. Suddenly, Vimes steps forward with the lantern.

VIMES
   Dr Cruces, I presume?

   (*Cruces pushes back his hood*)

Corporal Carrot here has a crossbow too. I'm not sure if he'd use it. He's a good man. I'm not. I'm nasty, mean and tired. Now then, Doctor. Perhaps you could explain what you're doing here? It can't be to look for Edward d'Eath, surely? Because our Corporal Nobbs has taken him off to the Watch Morgue, probably nicking any small items of personal jewellery he had on him, but that's just Nobby's way. I hope he's cleaned the clown make-up off him, poor chap.

I say this for old Nobby. He's got thieving hands and a criminal mind, but he hasn't got a criminal soul.

You used Edward, didn't you? He killed poor old Beano, and then he got the gonne, and he was there when it killed Hammerhock. And when he realised what was happening and came to you for advice . . . you killed him.

He couldn't have been the man up on the tower just now, not with the stab wound in his heart and all. I mean, I know that being dead isn't always a barrier to quiet enjoyment in this city, but I don't think young Edward's been up and about much.

The piece of cloth off his jacket was a nice touch. But you know, I've never believed in that kind of thing – neat clues, footprints in the flowerbeds and so on. Real policing's just slog and sweat. But lots of people would believe it. I mean, the body would be well preserved down here in the cool of the sewers. No-one would twig it'd beed dead too long. You'd just bring it out, dump it on the street and we'd have got the man who assassinated the Patrician.

DR CRUCES
You have no understanding. d'Eath was right, you know. About the monarchy.

VIMES
What about it, Dr Cruces?

(*Without warning, Cruces fires the gonne twice. Vimes and Carrot dive aside. Cruces takes a more dominant position on the stage*)

DR CRUCES
Stand up.

CARROT
Dr Cruces, I arrest you for the murder of Bjorn Hammerhock, Beano the clown, Edward d'Eath and Lance-Constable Cuddy of the City Watch.

DR CRUCES

Dear me. All those? I'm afraid you're right. Edward killed Brother Beano, the little fool. He said he didn't mean to. And I understand that Hammerhock was killed accidentally. He poked around, the charge fired and the bullet bounced off his anvil and killed him. That's what Edward said. He came to see me afterwards. Made a clean breast of the whole thing, you know. So I killed him. He was quite mad. There's no dealing with that sort of person. Stay back! He was babbling. He told me the gonne killed Hammerhock! On purpose! Hah! He said that the gonne was jealous! Hammerhock would have made more gonnes! Stop where you are! I had to kill Edward! He was a romantic, he would have got it wrong! But Ankh–Morpork does need a king!

But first, we have to get rid of you two!

(*He raises the gonne to fire it. There is a wolf howl. The werewolf appears, pushes Carrot out of the line of fire and turns towards Cruces. He fires twice. The werewolf falls to the floor. Carrot crosses to it. Vimes drops the crossbow and dives at Cruces. There is a struggle. Vimes gets control of the gonne*)

VIMES

I've got you now, you bastard!

DR CRUCES

Come, Captain. I'm an unarmed man.

(*He backs towards the fallen crossbow*)

VIMES

    Just give it up, Cruces. You can't get away.

    (*Keeping the gonne pointed at Cruces, he turns to Carrot*)

    How is she, Carrot?

      (*But in that moment, Cruces exits*)

    Carrot! Come on!

CARROT

    It's Angua, sir! He's killed her! She's dead, sir!

VIMES

    Corporal Carrot! Follow me! That's an order!

    (*He exits as the lights black out. Carrot remains over the body. The clocks start chiming twelve. If he's up to it, Carrot carries the werewolf off!*)

SCENE 24 – A ROOM IN THE ASSASSINS' GUILD

There is a desk, with some papers on it. Cruces enters. Vimes follows almost immediately. He points the gonne at Cruces.

VIMES
Got you. You're under arrest.

(*The gonne trembles in his hands*)

VOICE OF THE GONNE
Shoot him! Shoot him!

DR CRUCES
You can't shoot me. I know the law. So do you. You're a guard. You can't shoot me in cold blood.

VIMES (*lowering the gonne slightly*)
Yes. I am a guard. (*raising the gonne again*) But when those clocks stop chiming I won't be a guard any more.

VOICE OF THE GONNE
Shoot him. Shoot him now!

VIMES
We'll do it by the rules.

(The clocks stop chiming. Vimes raises the gonne to his shoulder, aiming it at Cruces' forehead. But now we hear the tinkling tune of Vimes' watch. Carrot enters)

CARROT

Put the gonne down, Captain. Put it down. Put it down now, Captain.

VIMES

You'll stop me, will you?

CARROT

Yes. Because it'll be murder.

VIMES

He killed Angua. Doesn't that mean anything to you?

CARROT

Yes. But personal isn't the same as important. *(pause)* Captain Vimes? Captain? Badge 177, Captain. It's never had more than dirt on it. Put down the gonne, Captain, you don't need it. *(suddenly barking out the order)* Put down that gonne, Watchman! Right now!

(Automatically, Vimes puts down the gonne and snaps to attention)

DR CRUCES

Listen! I'm sorry about . . . your friend. But there's evidence! It's here! All of it, sire! Edward was a fool. He didn't know what he'd found . . .

CARROT
I'm not interested.

DR CRUCES
The city needs a king!

CARROT
It does not need murderers.

DR CRUCES
But . . .

(*He dives for the gonne and scoops it up*)

It's all there, sire. Everything written down. Birthmarks and prophecies and genealogy and everything! Even your sword. It's the sword!

CARROT
Really? May I see?

(*He lowers his sword and crosses to the table*)

This is interesting.

(*He has his back to Cruces*)

DR CRUCES
Exactly. And now we must remove this annoying ex-policeman. (*to Vimes*) It's a shame, Vimes, if only you had . . .

(*He raises the gonne*)

CARROT
Dr Cruces?

(*As Cruces turns, Carrot stabs him*)

CRUCES
But why, sire? You could have been—

(*He dies*)

VIMES
Damn his hide! He . . . called you sire. What's in that—

CARROT (*picking up the gonne*)
You're late, Captain.

VIMES
Late?

CARROT
You were supposed to have been married (*he looks at Vimes' watch*) two minutes ago.

VIMES
Carrot . . .

CARROT
And you look a mess, sir. Got to get you cleaned up.

VIMES
Carrot . . . !

CARROT
Sir?

VIMES

I order you to give me those papers and the gonne.

CARROT

You can't order me. You're a civilian, now. A hot bath and a drink, sir. That's what you need. Let's go.

VIMES

A civilian? But this is my life.

(*Colon and Nobbs rush in*)

COLON

Captain! Corporal! Are you all right? Where's Angua?

VIMES

Dead.

CARROT

Gentlemen. Perhaps you'd be good enough to escort Captain Vimes back to his wedding.

VIMES

Carrot. Why did he call you sire? (*no reply*) You know, I could feel sorry for Cruces. The gonne changes people. We're all the same to the gonne. I'd have been just like him.

CARROT

No. You put it down, Captain.

VIMES
They call me Mister Vimes.

*(The others leave Carrot alone. A romantic version of
'Blue Moon' plays. Lights out)*

SCENE 25 – THE OBLONG OFFICE

The Patrician is on stage. There is a knock at the door.

PATRICIAN
  Come in, Corporal.

CARROT
  You were expecting me, my lord?

PATRICIAN
  Oh yes. What is it that you want me to do?

CARROT
  Sorry, sir, yes, to business . . . we could do with a new
  dartboard.

PATRICIAN
  I beg your pardon?

CARROT
  For when we're off-duty, you know. Helps the men
  relax.

PATRICIAN
  Another one? But you had one only last year!

CARROT
  It's the Librarian, sir. Nobby, er, Corporal Nobbs lets
  him play, sir. And what with him being an orang-utan,

he just reaches over from the oche and hammers the darts in. Ruins the board, see?

PATRICIAN
Very well. And . . . ?

CARROT
That's about it, sir. Apart from three new kettles.

PATRICIAN
Kettles as well? I'm sure you were awarded one for defeating the dragon last year. Why do you need three more?

CARROT
For the new arrangements, sir. (*opening a sheet of paper*) 'The Watch to be brought up to an establishment strength of fifty-six; the old Watch Houses at the River Gate, Deosil Gate and Hubwards Gate to be re-opened and manned on a 24-hour basis; a department for, er, looking at clues and things and dead bodies – so to start off with we'll probably need an alchemist and a ghoul, providing they promise not to take anything home and eat it. A request here from Corporal Nobbs that Watchmen be allowed all the weapons they can carry, although I'd be obliged if you said no to that one . . .

PATRICIAN
All right, all right. I can see how this is going. And supposing I say no?

CARROT
Do you know, sir, I never even considered that you'd say no?

171

PATRICIAN

Why not?

CARROT

It's all for the good of the city, sir. Do you know where the word 'policeman' comes from? It means 'man of the city'. From the old word polis . . .

PATRICIAN

Yes, thank you, Corporal. I did know that. (*pause*) It was bound to happen sooner or later. I accede to all your requests except the one involving Corporal Nobbs. And you, I think, should be promoted to Captain.

CARROT

Ye-es. I agree, sir. That would be a good thing for Ankh-Morpork. But I will not command the Watch, if that's what you mean.

PATRICIAN

Why not?

CARROT

Because I *could* command the Watch. Because . . . people should do things because an officer tells them. They shouldn't do it just because Corporal Carrot says so. Just because Corporal Carrot is . . . good at being obeyed.

PATRICIAN

An interesting point.

CARROT

But there used to be a rank, in the old days. Commander of the Watch. I suggest Samuel Vimes.

PATRICIAN

Oh yes. Commander of the Watch. The job became rather unpopular after the last post-holder beheaded Lorenzo the Kind. That man's name was Vimes, too. An ancestor, I suppose.

CARROT

Yes, sir. I looked it up.

PATRICIAN

Would he accept?

CARROT

Does a dragon explode in the woods, sir?

PATRICIAN

Does it?

CARROT

All the time. Not the same dragon every time, of course . . .

PATRICIAN

But you see . . . Captain, the trouble with Sam Vimes is that he upsets a lot of important people.

(*The Patrician and Carrot are suppressing the desire to grin*)

And I think that a Commander of the Watch would have to move in exalted circles, dine with the nobility, attend Guild functions . . . yes, I think I should rather enjoy seeing Vimes in that job.

CARROT
I'd taken the liberty, sir, of drafting a letter to the Cap . . . to Mr Vimes on your behalf. Just to save you trouble, sir.

PATRICIAN
You think of everything, don't you? (*he signs*) And is that the last of your dema . . . requests?

CARROT
Thank you, sir. That's all, I think.

PATRICIAN
Tell me, Captain . . . this business about there being an heir to the throne . . . What do you think about it?

CARROT
I don't think about it, sir. That's all sword-in-a-stone nonsense. Kings don't come out of nowhere, waving a sword and putting everything right. Everyone knows that.

PATRICIAN
But there was some talk of . . . evidence?

CARROT
No-one seems to know where it is, sir.

PATRICIAN

I wondered whether you might not have found it? In your investigations?

CARROT

I must have put it down somewhere. I'm sure I couldn't say where, sir.

PATRICIAN

My word. I hope you put it somewhere safe? With the gonne, perhaps? That seems to have vanished, too.

CARROT

I'm sure they're both well . . . guarded, sir.

PATRICIAN

Ah. Quite off the subject, of course . . . Constable Cuddy's funeral went well?

CARROT

Yes, sir. Buried in proper dwarfish tradition, sir.

PATRICIAN

Ye-es. They are generally buried with a weapon for use in the next world, I believe.

CARROT

I . . . really couldn't say, sir.

PATRICIAN

Ah. Buried deep, is he?

CARROT
  Yes, sir. A good, solid, coffin, sir.

PATRICIAN
  Good. Good. But . . . perhaps the city does need a king.
  Have you considered that?

CARROT
  Like a fish needs a . . . er . . . a thing that doesn't work
  underwater, sir.

PATRICIAN
  But a king can appeal to the emotions of his subjects,
  Captain. In . . . much the same way as you seem able to
  do.

CARROT
  Yes, sir. But what will he do next day? You can't treat
  people like puppet dolls. No, sir. Mr Vimes always says
  a man has got to know his own limitations. If there was a
  king, you know, incognito, then the best thing he could
  do would be to get on with a decent day's work.

PATRICIAN
  Indeed.

CARROT

  . . . But if there was a pressing need . . . then perhaps he'd
  think again. It's a bit like being a guard, really. When you
  need us, you really need us. And when you don't . . . well,
  best if we just walk around the streets and shout All's
  Well. Providing all is well, of course.

PATRICIAN
Well, I'll not keep you, Captain.

CARROT
Thank you, sir.

PATRICIAN
I was sorry to hear about Lance-Constable Angua.

CARROT
Thank you, my lord.

(*He turns to go*)

PATRICIAN
Captain? You're a man interested in words. I'd just invite you to consider something your predecessor never fully grasped.

CARROT
Sir?

PATRICIAN
You reminded me earlier that the word 'policeman' means 'man of the city'. Polis-man . . . Have you ever wondered where the word 'poli . . . tician' comes from?

(*Lights out*)

SCENE 26 – LADY RAMKIN'S HOUSE

Vimes and Lady Ramkin are on stage, sat at a table. Willikins stands behind the table. A grandfather clock can be heard ticking slowly. There is a silence, as Vimes puts a few peas from his plate into his mouth.

LADY RAMKIN
How are the peas, Sam?

VIMES
Oh . . . er . . . fine. Yes, fine.

LADY RAMKIN
I thought we might re-decorate the blue bedroom.

VIMES
Oh?

LADY RAMKIN
Yes. You know. As a nursery.

VIMES
Oh. Yes. (*he clears his throat*)

(*The doorbell goes. Willikins exits*)

LADY RAMKIN
Shall we make a start on dead-heading the roses tomorrow?

178

VIMES
Yes. Why not?

(*Willikins re-enters*)

WILLIKINS
Captain Carrot, sir.

VIMES
Captain?

(*Carrot enters and salutes*)

VIMES
It's all right, lad, you don't need to salute.

CARROT
Yes I do, sir.

(*He hands Vimes the envelope. Vimes opens it, and we hear Carrot's voice over the speakers*)

CARROT'S VOICE
'We are of a mind to increase the size of the City Watch to its old complement of fifty-six blah, blah, blah . . .

'We are also comma pleased to introduce pensions for the widows and orphans of Watchmen killed in the line of duty, feeling as you do that this is long overdue . . . blah, blah, blah . . .

'We consider particularly that comma this enlarged Watch will need an experienced man in charge who comma is held in Esteem by all parts of the society and comma we are convinced that you should fulfil this Roll full stop. You will therefore take up comma your Duties immediately as comma Commander of the Ankh-Morpork City Watch full stop. This post traditionally carries with it the rank of Knight which comma we are minded to resurrect on this one occasion full stop.

'Hoping this finds you in good health comma Yrs faithfully comma Havelock Vetinari brackets Patrician brackets'

(Vimes passes the letter to Lady Ramkin)

VIMES
But Corp . . . Captain Carrot!

CARROT
Sah!

VIMES
I . . .

LADY RAMKIN
My word! A knighthood? Not a moment too soon, either.

VIMES
Oh no! Not me! You know my views on the nobility – er, present company excepted, of course!

LADY RAMKIN
Then it's time the general stock was improved, then.

CARROT
His lordship did say that no part of the package was negotiable. All or nothing. All, Sir Samuel, or nothing.

VIMES
You've won, haven't you?

CARROT (*radiating honest ignorance*)
Sir Samuel? I don't understand.

VIMES
And you can stop calling me Sir Samuel, for a start. You tell the men they're to go on calling me 'the miserable old bastard', understand? Only now they're to do it where I can't hear them.

CARROT (*saluting*)
Yes, sir! You miserable old bastard, sir!

VIMES (*taking the letter*)
But it's ridiculous of course. There's no possible way I could oversee this sort of thing.

CARROT
What do you mean, sir?

VIMES
Well, look what it says here about reopening the Gatehouses. What's the point in that? Keep a general gate guard, yes, but if you're going to keep a finger on the pulse of . . . look, you'd need a Watch house along Elm Street, close to the Shades and the docks . . . look, give me a pencil and a notebook . . .

(We hear the following dialogue muttered under Lady Ramkin's and Carrot's conversation)

Yes, one halfway up Short Street, and maybe a smaller one in Kingsway. Somewhere up there, anyway. Got to think about population centres. Say six men per shift; the rest you'd move around on a monthly rota. Keep everyone on their toes. Ah, but we're taking over the Day Watch, too, and you've got to allow for days off, two grandmothers' funerals per year per man – gods know what we'll do about the undead, I suppose they get time off for their own funerals. Then there's sickness and so on . . .

LADY RAMKIN *(gently ushering Carrot out)*
Well, done, Captain. He was beginning to get very miserable. Of course, he was very gloomy as a guard, but at least he enjoyed it.

CARROT
Yes, Ma'am!!

LADY RAMKIN
Captain . . . I was very sorry to hear about Angua.

CARROT
Thank you, my lady. I . . . thank you.

(Carrot walks out of the scene into a pool of light. He stands there, for a second. Then Angua enters and crosses to him. They embrace, gently)

I wasn't certain. But I thought, well, isn't it only silver that kills them? I just had to hope.

ANGUA

Carrot . . . I know that you have a problem with . . . the undead . . .

CARROT

Well . . . I've been thinking about that. I think maybe the only prejudices a man's got the right to have are the ones he earns. Anyway I've got you for three weeks out of every four. And for the other seven days . . . well, at least I'll have someone who's always ready for a nice long walk!

(*They embrace and turn to walk upstage as the curtain falls*)

THE END

MEN AT ARMS – PROPS LIST

On the furniture side, we just had a bed, plus a small table and some multi-purpose chairs (the Watch house, Vimes'/Carrot's rooms, etc). We re-used the door-with-a-hole-in that we'd built for the doorknocker in *Mort* by adding a gold-painted plastic 'boob' from a joke shop – fitted with a water supply so that it could fire at Colon and Nobbs. We also had, on set throughout, Cornice-Overlooking-Broadway.

Property	Scene Where First Used	Used By
Klaxon on Pole	1	Footnote
Letter of Resignation	2	Patrician
Axe	2	Cuddy
Clipboard	2	Colon
Fag-end	2	Nobby
Sword	2	Carrot
Lectern	3	On Stage
Three Coins	3	Colon
Trick 'Iron' Bar	4	Edward
Scythe	4	Death
Legal Document	5	Morecombe
Grubby Hanky	5	Vimes

Property	Scene Where First Used	Used By
Cup of Klatchian Coffee	14	Cuddy
Bath Back-brush	15	Willikins
Bath (we used a cut-out)	15	On Stage
Vimes' Watch	16	Carrot
Custard Pies	17	The Watch
Morningstar	17	Nobby
Squirty Flower	17	Dr Whiteface
Painted Egg	17	Boffo
Paper & Quill Pen	19	Carrot
Sheet	19	Angua
Bouquet	20	Lady Ramkin
Strip of Black Cloth	22	Cuddy
Pistol Crossbows	23	Vimes, Carrot
Lantern	23	Vimes
Paperwork (Evidence)	24	Dr Cruces
Letter & Pen	25	Carrot
Plates of Peas (& Cutlery, etc)	26	On Stage

**TERRY PRATCHETT'S
GUARDS! GUARDS!**
The play
adapted by Stephen Briggs

'Alle Thee Dysk's a Stage'

Terry Pratchett's infamous city of Ankh-Morpork is under threat from a 60 foot fire-breathing dragon, summoned by a secret society of malcontented tradesmen.

Defending Ankh-Morpork against this threat is the entire, underpaid, under-valued City Night Watch - a drunken and world-weary Captain, a cowardly and overweight Sergeant, a small opportunistic Corporal of dubious parentage . . . and their newest recruit, Lance-Constable Carrot, who is upright, literal, law-abiding and keen. Aiding them in their fight for truth, justice and the Ankh-Morporkian way are a small swamp dragon and the Librarian of Unseen University (who just happens to be an orangutan).

Stephen Briggs has been involved in amateur dramatics for over 25 years and he assures us that the play can be staged without needing the budget of Industrial Light and Magic. Not only that, but the cast should still be able to be in the pub well before closing time.

Oh, and a word of advice omitted from the play text:

LEARN THE WORDS   (Havelock, Lord Vetinari)

0 552 14431 2

THE DISCWORLD NOVELS OF TERRY PRATCHETT

THE FUNNIEST AND MOST UNORTHODOX FANTASIES IN THIS OR ANY OTHER GALAXY

MASKERADE

The show must go on, as murder, music and mayhem run riot in the night . . .

The Opera House, Ankh-Morpork . . . a huge, rambling building, where innocent young sopranos are lured to their destiny by a strangely-familiar evil mastermind in a hideously-deformed evening dress . . .

At least, he hopes so. But Granny Weatherwax, Discworld's most famous witch is in the audience. *And she doesn't hold with that sort of thing.*

So there's going to be *trouble* (but nevertheless a good evening's entertainment with murders you can really hum . . .)

'Pratchett is as funny as Wodehouse and as witty as Waugh'
Independent

Maskerade is the eighteenth novel in the now legendary *Discworld* series.

0 552 14236 0

A LIST OF OTHER TERRY PRATCHETT
TITLES AVAILABLE FROM CORGI BOOKS

THE PRICES SHOWN BELOW WERE CORRECT AT THE TIME OF GOING TO PRESS. HOWEVER, TRANSWORLD PUBLISHERS RESERVE THE RIGHT TO SHOW NEW RETAIL PRICES ON COVERS WHICH MAY DIFFER FROM THOSE PREVIOUSLY ADVERTISED IN THE TEXT OR ELSEWHERE.

All Transworld titles are available by post from:

Book Service By Post, P.O. Box 29, Douglas, Isle of Man IM99 1BQ

Credit cards accepted. Please telephone 01624 675137, fax 01624 670923, Internet http://www.bookpost.co.uk or e-mail: bookshop@enterprise.net for details.

Free postage and packing in the UK. Overseas customers: allow £1 per book (paperbacks) and £3 per book (hardbacks).